Cut Throat

By K. Roland Williams

Compilation and Introduction copyright © 2008 by
Triple Crown Publications
PO Box 6888
Columbus, Ohio 43205
www.TripleCrownPublications.com

Library of Congress Control Number: 2008922681
ISBN 13: 978-0-9799517-3-2
Author: K. Roland Williams
Photography, Cover Design/Graphics:
  www.TreagenPhotography.com
Typesetting: Holscher Type and Design
Associate Editor: Eliza Jane Wood
Editor-in-Chief: Mia McPherson
Consulting: Vickie M. Stringer

First Trade Paperback Edition Printing March 2008

10 9 8 7 6 5 4 3 2

Printed in Canada

dedication

This book is dedicated to the loving memory of my father, Kenneth Roland Williams Sr., who taught me how to survive in these streets and to always try to be an equal balance of strength and compassion.

Rest in Peace -- you are not forgotten.

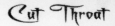

acknowledgements

First and foremost, I have to thank GOD for giving me the talents that I have to express myself in so many creative ways. Thank you for protecting me from the death that has surrounded me for so many years of my life. I know I shouldn't be here now. Please continue to show me my purpose in life. I will wait for you.

To my mother Arlene Williams (my favorite lady) who sacrificed so much to make sure I had everything I needed and wanted, and never missed a meal. Even when we didn't have it she made it happen—you are my rock and foundation. I love you!

To my three big sisters: Charlene, Libby and Elaine. All three of you have contributed to me growing into a man whether you realize it or not. I love you and thank you for all that you have taught me.

Charlene- you taught me to have faith and think like an entrepreneur.

Libby- you introduced me to class and sophistication.

Elaine- your gift to me has been the importance of living life to its fullest.

You are all fearless, and I admire you more than you know.

To my beautiful children:

I love you more than life itself, and let this book stand as evidence that you can be and do anything that you put your mind to. Let no man tell you otherwise! You are my future, hopes and dreams.

K. Roland Williams

vii

To Dominique "Niki" Norris, Danielle and Tierney, my three nieces, I love you all deeply. Can you help me push these books in the Burgh, North Carolina and Atlanta? Let's all get dat paper!

To the mean streets of Homewood and the Hill District in my hometown of Pittsburgh, PA. You helped make and mold me, and in a way if it wasn't for the adversity I faced growing up in those streets, I wouldn't have the strength and wisdom that I have today, nor would I have any stories to share with the world.

Special shout out to my cuz Cecily Chavis Martin and her Virginia clan. I miss your smile and advice. Let's do a better job of keeping in touch.

Much love goes out to Dame and Jules — keep the hip hop alive and keep writing those flows and hot tracks. Shake off the haters, and focus on your craft. Your day is coming!

Thanks to Triple Crown for giving me an opportunity to express myself through a pen and pad. Thank you Mia for your help and guidance throughout this process.

And special thanks go to Vickie Stringer for your perseverance and foresight to start TCP. Without you, new authors would not have a venue to write and be heard. Quincy thanks you as well for allowing him to have a chance to breathe and be introduced to the world.

Special appreciation goes out to my friend, TCP author Toy Styles (Black and Ugly and a Hustler's Son) who has given me more advice than anyone about this writing game. You are a great writer and visionary and I know that everything you pen will be fire! We have to write something together real soon!

Much appreciation also goes to TCP authors Cynthia White

K. Roland Williams

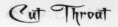
and Dawn Desiree for being really good friends and encouraging me while I was waiting for my book to drop. May all that you write hit the best seller's list!

Thank you Eliza (my editor) for giving me your recommendations and advice while making it appear that I actually had an option in the creative process — smile. You have helped me take the book from good to great.

Thanks to my junior editors who supplied their opinion of the manuscript in the early drafts — Ty, Hope and Samantha. Special appreciation goes to all of you for your help and advice.

To the rest of my family and the few peeps that I call friends, I haven't forgotten you. You have all contributed to my life in ways that words can never express. I value you all.

To Lynn, Tina, Dre, Mo, Mel, Eric Cherry, Aunt Marie and all of the Givner clan — thanks for being who you are.

To C.S.Brown: You have been my muse and inspiration. Without you, I may not have mustered the desire to complete the manuscript. You supplied me with strength when I was weak and light when I was surrounded by darkness. I was <u>Lost without You</u>. You helped me through the most difficult time of my life and I will always appreciate you for that. No matter what the future holds, you will remain a fixture in the most sacred place in my heart. Nothing can ever take that away.

And last but certainly not least, to all of the haters out there, a special note — Keep hatin'. It's because of people like you that keep people like me on my toes and grindin'!

Enjoy the novel...

K. Roland Williams

ix

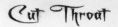

one

Quincy Underwood stood in the center of the square stage bathed in the glow of colorful spotlights. As he peered out over the crowded nightclub, his bedroom eyes and sexy, slanted grin silently seduced the women sitting at the small, round, linen-clad tables that skirted the dance floor and stage.

Q's warm, soulful riffs were melodic, poignant and controlled, giving him a unique mix of smooth Rhythm and Blues and Neo Soul to claim as his own style. His band, Taboo, backed him expertly. Through the gray wisps of cigarette smoke and dim, candle-lit ambiance of The Melody Room, Quincy could see that with every crescendo and key change, he had the crowd once again in the palm of his hand.

After the band's last set of the evening, some of the women made their rounds, giving warm, affectionate hugs to the band members, flirting and eagerly passing cell phone numbers without shame. Quincy flirted with a few of the women and discreetly scooped up no less than three phone numbers. He noted that the last girl he spoke to was going to have to be put on the top of his Get Wit' list. She whispered something in his ear about giving him some bomb-ass head at the end of the night—if, of course, he would accept.

Q glanced down at the name and number she had scribbled on a small piece of scrap paper—Valerie. Q smiled at the unbelievable power that being on the stage and in the limelight gave him. Valerie, with her fat ass, chinky eyes and full lips, was a dime fo' real, and if he could sneak away for a minute and meet up with this chick in his ride for some dome, it was gonna have to be on. *Damn, I ain't even got a record deal yet,* Quincy thought. *Imagine the pussy that will line up for me once I do!*

He stepped away to grab a drink and watched the band pack the gear up for the night. Robert, the band's keyboardist and background vocalist, started to break the gear down, coiling the cables tightly into their cases like lifeless black snakes. He and Quincy had been boys for years and played together in local bands ever since high school. Robert was married, and that nigga refused to fuck around on his wife, Cathy. After the shows, his ass went straight to the crib, no fuckin' around with any of the club groupies.

Marcel, the band's drummer, was a very different story altogether. You couldn't keep his pussy-chasin' ass

K. Roland Williams

away from the ladies. Shit, to Marcel, the club was like a Get Pussy Free card. He wasn't the best-looking cat by any means, with his droopy eyes and beer gut, but the nigga did keep everybody laughing. He was funny as shit and fun to kick it with. In the music business, even the ugliest cat got his share of pussy, even if it was sloppy seconds.

The last member of Taboo was Xavier Patterson. Quincy and Xavier had known each other for several years, and Q considered him his boy—blood in, blood out. They had been there for each other through a lot of crazy shit. Quincy thought back on the latest drama several months back when Xavier was caught at his jump-off Brandi's house when her husband came home early from work. Quincy had to chuckle to himself at the thought of X trapped in Brandi's closet whispering into his cell phone butt-ass naked.

Brandi's husband was a cop for D.C. Metro and X, needing to escape, called Quincy from the closet to somehow come and bail him out. Quincy thought, *niggaz sure do some stupid-ass shit to get at a hot piece of ass.* Q didn't have a clue what he could do to help his boy out of his sticky situation, but he'd rushed over to Brandi's crib anyway to try to find a way to get her husband out of the bedroom and to the front door so that X could slip out the back window. After a few minutes of stuttering and making up a lie that Q was looking for a friend and thought he lived there at Brandi's crib, Xavier

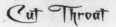
slid out the back, jumped down into the yard half naked and 'bout broke his neck in the process. *Now that,* Quincy thought to himself, *was some funny-ass shit. Yeah, those were the good ol' days,* he reminisced.

Lately though, shit was nothing like that. Q and his boy had been growing apart and going their separate ways more and more every day. Quincy figured that they would work it out eventually, but it felt like a large piece of their friendship was being chipped away like concrete from a broken sidewalk. Soon, there would be nothing left but dust and old memories.

Right at that moment, as if X knew Quincy was thinking of him, he noticed his boy staring from across the bar. Q acted as if he didn't see his glaring, penetrating looks and ignored Xavier altogether. Quincy thought it might have been his relationship with Neecy, the new fine-ass bartender, that had X acting like a bitch. The second Neecy walked her thick, curvaceous ass through the club's front door three months earlier, Xavier had his mind made up that she would be his. But apparently, she had other ideas. Shit, all was fair in love and war, and she had chosen Quincy. They had been kicking it off and on ever since. More off than on, but X didn't know that.

Xavier watched Neecy and Quincy interact often. He would sit there at the bar between sets all somber and shit, drinking his Crown Royal and smoking Newports like they were going out of style. Looking like a little-ass kid who had lost his fuckin' puppy. There were tons of

K. Roland Williams

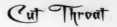

women in the club, all shapes and sizes, and he was fixated on this particular one.

Xavier came over to talk to Quincy with a drink in his hand and his brows furrowed, looking pissed off about something.

"Oh shit, here we go," Quincy said under his breath.

"You were a little off with that two-part harmony on the back end of the last song." Xavier could have been Quincy's baby brother; he was just a few inches shorter and a shade of chocolate lighter, with the same muscular build and confident swagger. He looked Quincy up and down awaiting a response.

"What's up, bruh? You say I was off on the harmonies?" Quincy leaned into his boy, acting like he couldn't hear X over the bass of the music that the DJ had blasting over the club's sound system.

"I said your harmonies were like shit tonight."

Quincy gritted his teeth and cut his eyes sharply at Xavier. "You're joking, right? My harmonies were tight tonight. Those changes I made last rehearsal sounded fine to me."

"The changes *you* made? You mean *our* vocal arrangement." Xavier slid in close to Quincy's ear. "Yo, bruh, you and me ... we need to have a little talk. There are a few things that I have to get off my chest. Now is as good a time as any to do it." Xavier seemed to be sizing Quincy up; his finger was like a dagger pointing into Q's broad chest.

K. Roland Williams

Quincy inhaled deeply to keep himself calm. He could smell the cigarettes and liquor on Xavier's breath. He chalked the shit up to X having a bad night. He tried to make sense of the whole thing without it leading to something ugly, but his patience was wearing thin as rice paper.

"Yeah, what's up? What's on your mind, homie?" Quincy asked, meeting Xavier's gaze to show that he wasn't afraid to get into any type of confrontation with him. X escorted Quincy to a corner of the club away from the massive speakers, trying to find a small pocket of relative quiet to relieve the burden that tugged hard on his conscience.

"Oh shit," Quincy exclaimed as he looked down at his boy's wrist, distracted. "Where in the hell did you get that watch? Is that a knock-off?"

Xavier responded with an arrogant look as if he had forgotten he had the watch, throwing his wrist up toward the club's lights, just a few inches away from Quincy's face. "Knock off my ass, nigga, this is a six-thousand-dollar timepiece."

"Exactly my point, X, where'd you get it?" Quincy's curiosity was getting the best of him, trying to put off the conversation that he knew was inevitable.

"Erhhh, you know I collect watches. I saved up for it. Anyway, why you grilling me like you an interrogator or some shit?"

"Relax. Damn, nigga, I was just asking."

K. Roland Williams

Before the two could start their conversation, a small group of men approached from the far side of the dance floor to speak to the two singers, interrupting them. A short man in a black suit and bright red tie led the well-dressed group.

"Yo, Quincy, you sounded great tonight, we wanted to thank you for ummm, putting the ladies in the proper romantic mood and holla at you about singing at my man's wedding, if you have a minute." He pointed to the man on his right who was proudly smiling, but obviously drunk. "We've been trying to talk his dumb ass out of getting hitched, but he insists on doing it anyway." The men broke out into a round of liquor-driven laughter, the two-for-one happy hour drinks clearly catching up with them.

Quincy hesitated and looked at Xavier with that familiar look his boy knew so well. Q was relieved that he didn't have to talk to X. He wasn't in the mood for the drama tonight. "Let me talk to these dudes for a minute, I'll holla at you later."

Xavier faked a tight-lipped grin, glanced down at his new platinum and diamond Breitling watch and gave up. He was used to Quincy getting all of the attention, despite the fact that Xavier had run the band and had been lead vocalist just last year, back when Raymond had stepped in and suggested that the group put the pretty boy in as lead vocalist. Quincy's adlib and riff skills were far more advanced than Xavier's were, and Q was quickly voted lead vocalist by the rest of the band. X still resented him for it but knew it wasn't entirely his fault— no one dared question Raymond's authority. His suggestions were never simply that, no matter how nicely he put it. What he said was the final word and everyone knew it.

Quincy continued talking to the group of men while Xavier looked on impatiently from a distance.

"Same old fuckin' Quincy." Xavier shook his head and gritted his teeth.

From that exact moment, he didn't see Q as his boy anymore. Naw, he was just a nigga out to get his. So X figured fuck it, he may as well just look out for himself, too.

Xavier shook his head while he walked away. "Some shit never changes. That's the last time any nigga's gonna shit on me and get away wit' it."

Δ Δ Δ Δ

DJ Turbo, armed with two iPods connected to a serious MIDI sound system, began hyping up the crowd. He played the latest Top Twenty hits and brought the club to life, changing the sexy mood that the band had set to party mode, quickly filling the dance floor with crowds of people ready to get their swerve on.

After agreeing to consider singing at the man's wedding, Quincy slipped away from the crowd and sat alone

K. Roland Williams

in the corner at the neon and block-glass bar. He figured he would get back with X later, but right now he needed to get his head right and have a drink. Swirling a straw around his Grey Goose and cranberry, he admired Neecy from a distance and still caught the occasional glimpse of Xavier in his peripheral vision, watching blankly, his eyes glazed over like frosted glass, plotting and scheming.

Δ Δ Δ Δ

Quincy preferred his women thick with generous curves, a quick wit and a good sense of humor, and Neecy fit the bill to a T. She had been blessed with a million-dollar smile and equally gorgeous ass, and Q lustfully scanned every inch of her frame. They had been out to dinner a few times already, and he knew from the beginning that she was wifey material. Neecy wasn't anything like the chicks Q had dated over the years. She was one of those good ol' bring-home-to-your-mother type of chicks. The type to settle down and have a shit-load of babies with. The kind of woman that you had to respect because she respected herself. No ass on the first date ... second, third or fourth, for that matter, and Q wasn't used to that shit at all.

He was used to having a woman all over his ass from day one. He had the looks, the body and the swagger, plus the nigga could sing, too! That was what usually got him into the panties. He would find a song that the girl liked and lay the shit down for her at the right moment. From that point, she would be all wet in the panties and would eventually give in. No matter how long she originally said she would wait—it would be a wrap, the pussy would belong to him!

That was where Neecy was very different. She wasn't any innocent religious type, she did let Quincy kiss her and squeeze her big-ass titties in the movie a little bit, but that was where her freakiness ended. Quincy tried to push the envelope at first, but when she said not yet, she meant that shit, and Quincy had to deal with that. She was a challenge, and Q had always appreciated a challenge.

Quincy saw her serving the club's patrons drinks at the far end of the bar. Every so often, she glanced his way and shot him a smile or a wink. She sashayed toward Quincy as if for that moment, they were the only two people in the club. Her slim waist gave way to curvy hips and thighs, and Quincy focused on every cat-like step she took.

"Damn ... she is fine." He wiped his brow with a napkin from the bar.

While he checked Neecy out, she admired his sharp black linen two-piece outfit, which, she noted, wrapped nicely around his well-built chest. The vest-style top he sported exposed his muscular arms and the complicated black tribal-pattern tattoo that encircled the shoulder,

K. Roland Williams

biceps and triceps of his right arm.

"That nigga know he fine," she said to herself in a pursed whisper as she moved toward him, shaking her head and smiling like the Cheshire cat from *"Alice in Wonderland."* She temporarily neglected the droves of thirsty and impatient patrons who were crowded around the bar awaiting service, twenty dollar bills waving and flapping in the air like small green flags, trying to get her attention. Surrendering a flirtatious smile, her dimples dipped into mocha-colored cheeks while her lips curled at the fringes of her heart-shaped face. She wore her hair back proudly in long black braids cinched neatly into a ponytail. The only jewelry that adorned her was a small diamond solitaire on her right hand, the remnants of a failed engagement.

"By the way, you and the band sounded great tonight." The twang of her Southern accent was powerful and melodic, commanding Q's undivided attention. Her drawl was a dramatic departure from the slang of southeastern D.C., Quincy's old stomping ground.

"Thanks, baby girl," he replied as he slowly sipped his drink, glancing down every few seconds to admire the roundness of her double D's through the tight T-shirt.

"You gonna get cussed out in a minute. Everybody's waiting on you to make them drinks ... niggaz tryin' to get they drink on and you holdin' up progress," Quincy said with a smirk.

"Let 'em wait," she said with much attitude over the

music. "I ain't a damn stripper to be waving money at, especially when it ain't going into *my* pocket."

"Damn, did you put any *cranberry* in this glass?" he complained with an exaggerated cough and gag.

She cut the man a sarcastic look across the bowl of untouched peanuts on the bar. "Stop complaining and enjoy your drink. I made it extra strong for you."

He smiled and sipped at the narrow straw again.

"That's better. I'll be back in a few minutes, all right?" She bolted off to grab a Budweiser for a tall slim brotha decked out in a bright blue hat and matching suit and gators.

Neecy passed out the round of mixed drinks, beers and coolers, quickly returning to the side of the bar where Quincy still sat patiently.

"If I didn't know any better, *Miss* Neecy," he began, "I would think that you were trying to get me drunk. Maybe so you can take advantage of me later?"

"Ha! You wish. I don't need to get you tipsy, Quincy," she quipped. "Besides, I want you sober and thinking straight if and when I ever bless you with some of this luscious shit." She turned to the side, purposely showing off the full roundness of her ass. The cat in the Baby Phat logo was stretched to its sewn limits.

"Daaamn girl, you know you wrong for dat shit."

"Yeah, I know, but you like it anyway. If you can break away from your groupies long enough for us get to know each other, who knows where this *friendship* of

K. Roland Williams

ours could go ... it's like I got to compete with the entire club for your attention. Even the times we went out, every chick in the street knew you, flirtin' and what not. But it's cool, I understand you got to do your thang, and believe me, I can respect that." She rolled her neck and crossed her arms awaiting the man's response, her MAC lip gloss shining in the lights.

It must be the Southern upbringing, Quincy thought, that made Neecy so different from the other women he dated most of his life. All he knew was, he was highly attracted to her, and not just her body, but her conversation, which was a very new feeling for the life-long player and pretty boy. She was a hard worker and was in George Washington University studying nursing with serious plans for her future, and Q admired that in her. She said she worked as a bartender just to get through school, and he really liked the fact that she had principles and wouldn't do anything that might compromise her morals.

If it weren't for the music and Q's commitment to becoming a star, he would most definitely try to settle down, and this one—Neecy—could get the diamond ring on her finger. As usual though, it was just the wrong time for Quincy, and love beat a hasty getaway like a bandit robbing a bank. *One day,* he thought ... *just not today.*

Quincy thought about how his momma would like Neecy. Right before she passed of cancer, his mother told him to try to settle down and leave all those fast-ass little hussies alone. Q could still hear the respirator beeping and smell the sterile aroma of ammonia in the freezing hospital room. She died alone with no one there in that dank-ass room, and Quincy never forgave himself for not visiting her that day so long ago. He dry washed his face in his hands and abandoned the sad thoughts of his mother and turned his attention back to Neecy.

"I wouldn't call them groupies," he said humbly, trying to wipe his mother's smile from his mind, "and I do have to do my *thang* as you put it, but that don't mean I can't keep finding time for you. Believe me, we'll see each other again real soon. I invited you to the crib a few times, and you keep shootin' me down, shit ... a black man can only handle so much rejection. You won't come to my apartment, I can't go to yours. In fact, you always have me drop you off at the door and shit. What if something happens to you? I could at least walk you to the apartment couldn't I?"

"Yeah, I know what you're sayin', Quincy, but I also know what can happen if we get carried away when we're alone. I see the way you look at me," she joked, batting her long eyelashes. "Always undressing me with those big brown eyes of yours."

"Look, Neecy, this is what's up. I'll be a gentlemen from the beginning to the end, you have nothing to be worried about. I'll show you how we D.C. brothas get

K. Roland Williams

down. Oh, and by the way, I see the way *you* look at *me*, too."

"What?" she said with a sly grin. "The way I look at you?"

"Yeah girl, the way you look at me. Whether you come over to my pad or I come to yours, it's all good. You'll be treated with respect ... as long as you never wear those tight-ass jeans again." He reached across the bar toward Neecy's thick tail. Neecy pushed him playfully.

"I'll even sing for you. Any song you want." Q flashed a perfect smile and gave Neecy his most sincere look.

"All right, I'll hold you to that, and when the time is right, we'll see what happens. Oh, and by the way, what makes you think *I* was worried about *you* doing something to *me*?" The look in her brown, almond-shaped eyes read as genuine; Quincy knew she was feeling him.

"Look, Quincy," she said, her eyes narrowed and her usual voice faded into a faint, secretive whisper, almost a pant, as she took on a completely different demeanor. Her normal welcoming purr took on a more callous quality, one that Quincy didn't quite recognize. She moved in close to Q's ear. Her warm breath was sweet, Q noted, just like strawberry licorice.

"When was the last time you spoke to the big boss?" Her eyes washed over Quincy's face, probing for more than simple words, she was searching for answers.

"Who, Raymond? I try to avoid that dangerous-ass

nigga every chance I get, why … what's up, what do you need to know?"

"I don't know, I'm just a little curious as to what's *really* going on here behind the scenes. I've heard some crazy shit lately, and I don't want to get caught up in anything without all the facts. Shit can get real wild behind this bar."

"What do you mean by crazy … crazy is an everyday thing around here, what … you didn't know?"

"Well, talk around here is that Raymond James and his boys are big time hustlers and killers." She glanced up occasionally to Ray's upper office window. "I just want to know what I got myself into coming to work here for him." She looked at Quincy with a sort of innocence, like a woman opening up a round of gossip with a table full of giddy, tipsy girlfriends.

Quincy's eyebrow ascended with curiosity at her unpredictable change in subject and sudden interest in the owner of the nightclub. Moving in closer to the woman's ear, he returned her whispers over the music. "Neecy, I know that you're new here and don't really know how shit works yet, being from Atlanta and new to D.C. Let me put a bug in yo' ear so that you know what's up. You have to be very, very careful 'bout what questions you ask around here and who hears you ask 'em. There are eyes and ears everywhere that report back to Raymond. And make sure you never ever, *under any circumstances*, say a word around that crooked-ass nigga

Kane, Ray's nephew. That nigga think he the next Tony Montana."

"Yeah, I can tell, now what's *his* story?" She asked the question with wide eyes and her head low, chin almost to her chest.

"You sure do have a bunch of questions all of a sudden. You writing a book or some shit? Bottom line is, Ray and his peoples is knee deep in the game, and niggaz that know anything about D.C. know not to bring any drama in here fuckin' wit' Ray's club, so you don't have anything to worry about." Quincy stood and pushed away from the bar. "We'll talk a little later. Like I said, I'll make the time."

"Smooches," she whispered under her breath as she impassively watched Quincy disappear into the crowd.

two

Tristan Kendall Grant, a.k.a. Kane, sat behind the rich wood-grain steering wheel of his pearl white Cadillac Escalade in the rear lot of The Melody Room. He slowly bobbed his head to the low thumping of his Alpine's bass, watching keenly from a distance as cars pulled into the already jammed front parking lot. The lot attendants packed them into the spaces like sardines.

One of Kane's soldiers sat in the passenger's seat while a second man sat behind him in the massive back seat. Security waved folks over to a second parking lot across the street, where the Giant Eagle grocery store and shopping center stood. It worked nicely as the club's overflow lot on nights like this one, when Ray's spot was jam-packed.

The car that Kane awaited slowly pulled up. Its slanted amber fog lights resembled angry eyes on a prowling cat. The small Lexus convertible carried two men inside, both serious gangsters by the look of them, and they

K. Roland Williams

were not there to party. They had come to do business. That business was to buy several keys of the purest coke on the East Coast: Raymond's cocaine.

Security knew exactly who to look for and who to allow access to the private gated area in the rear of the club. The security guard waved the flashlight toward Kane's truck to verify that they were the right men. Kane flashed his headlights twice, the signal for the car to approach the corner of the empty rear lot.

Once the Lexus pulled up, it came to a stop several car lengths away from the truck, engine still idling, and the two men stepped cautiously outside into the warm, sticky summer night air. One of the men, the taller of the two, reached into his suit jacket to indicate that he was strapped and ready to pull heat if Kane and his soldiers got sheisty. He spoke quietly to his partner and a gold tooth sparkled in the parking lot lights. Both men were well-dressed and appeared experienced in this type of business, but Kane still felt uneasy about the transaction.

This was a deal that Ray had made through a third party. Kane had been thoroughly against this particular piece of business—it went against his gangster sixth sense—but Ray was the boss, and what his Uncle Ray said was the law. No one dared question Raymond's authority, not unless they wanted to end up fish food in the Potomac River. Ray's hasty decision to do business with these two unknown cats from the Midwest put

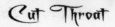

Kane on the defensive, and as far as Kane was concerned, these two country-ass bamas were five-o. He did not want to take any chances.

"You two niggaz keep your eyes open and fuckin' mouths closed, I do the talking," Kane briefed the two youngins who sat in the truck with him. "If either of those two clowns makes any moves, smoke they asses right here in the lot. Do not hesitate!"

"Which one of you two is Remy?" Kane asked as he and his two inexperienced soldiers exited the truck, stopping dead center of the two vehicles' opposing lights.

"I am. Are you Kane?"

"That's right."

"Why'd you pick this crowded-ass club to do business in? You couldn't find a more private place?"

"What difference does the place make? Besides, we do this quick and easy, and we just look like a bunch of cats talking shit in the parking lot of a busy nightclub. We get this thing done fast and we all on our merry fuckin' way."

"So," Kane continued, "did you bring the money or what?"

"Yeah, of course, you don't think we came all this way just to talk to your ass tonight, do you?"

"Whatever, nigga ... let's see the dough." Kane stepped away from the truck and closer to the men.

Remy motioned to the other man to get the money.

K. Roland Williams

His partner reached carefully into the small back seat of the convertible and pulled out a large Pacers basketball duffle bag. Remy nodded his head and gave his approval for his partner to throw Kane the bag. The bag landed hard at Kane's feet, thudding against the asphalt of the parking lot and throwing up a small blanket of dust that settled on his six-hundred-dollar gators. Kane looked down at his now-dusty shoes and back up at the man who threw the bag. The grimace on Kane's face was evident, which made the man who threw the bag smile, obviously pleased with his ability to affect Kane with such a simple thing.

To further annoy Kane, the man with Remy said, "Don't worry, you can afford a new pair now."

Kane bit his lip, deciding to give the nigga a pass for the sake of business, and lifted the bag, unzipped it and carefully analyzed its contents. He counted the banded five-thousand-dollar bundles aloud, "Eighty, ninety, a-hundid." Appearing satisfied, he smiled.

"It's all there," Remy said, "one hundred grand." Pulling out a cigarette and lighter from his jacket pocket, he snapped open the Zippo with a metallic clack, lit up and pulled deep on the Newport; plumes of smoke circling his neat dreadlocks.

Kane motioned for his soldier to retrieve *their* duffle bag. It wasn't stashed inside of the luxury truck, but in the tall, well-trimmed bushes next to the air conditioning unit behind the club. This was small weight, but

Kane still felt uncomfortable about these strangers he had never done business with before.

While Kane and his boys were preoccupied, Remy quietly pulled out a switchblade from his pocket and fingered the release button. The blade ejected with a sharp snap. One of Kane's young thugs walked over to Remy and threw him the full satchel.

Remy reached inside of the bag and cut a small slit into one of the five bundles of white powder. He removed a small sample of the cocaine from one of the kilos and, balancing the powder on the tip of his knife, dropped the product into a small, liquid-filled vial. The chemical reaction of the two substances turned the liquid dark blue, proving that it was definitely pure yayo.

"We good, nigga, or what?" Kane was getting impatient with the man's chemistry experiment.

"Yeah, we good ... shit, real fuckin' good." Remy smiled to his partner, plucking the vial with the middle finger of his right hand, and holding it up into the parking lot lights with another.

"A'ight, that means we're done here," Kane said. "Good doing business with you."

As Kane backed up toward his truck, Remy yelled out, "Oh yeah, and tell your boss we want to double this amount on the re-up. Ten birds, no less. But we need to meet with him on that shit, or we go to the Columbians directly."

"Shit, whatever, nigga, go wherever the fuck you

K. Roland Williams

need to go. Ten bricks ain't shit. You actin' like yaw big time and shit. You see the man when you up your buy," Kane said sucking his teeth. "I ain't making no promises to you about shit."

"You gonna pass the message, errand boy, or do I have to contact your boss myself and tell him you about to fuck up a quarter-million-dollar deal? Do you think he'll like that idea?" Remy's partner looked grimly at Kane and his two boys. He was clearly the muscle of the duo, and he waited for the tension in the conversation to build for an excuse to pull his gun.

"What you just call me ... errand boy?" Kane's voice echoed in the small rear lot of the club as if the devil himself had spoken the words. "Nigga, you got me all fucked up! Let me show you what kind of *errand* I'm 'bout to run on yo' ass!" Kane quickly pulled the nine millimeter out of the front of his jeans and cocked the slide back, mechanically feeding a hollow point into the receiver.

Remy's bodyguard did the same along with the two young thugs with Kane. All guns were locked, loaded and threatening to go off at any second.

"I ain't 'fraid of no gun, nigga! I was puttin' caps in little bitch-ass niggaz like you when you was a snot-nose kid!" Kane thumbed the button on the handle of his nine, the infrared beam materializing and dancing nervously across Remy's chest.

"Tell yo' boy to put his heat down," Kane command-

K. Roland Williams

ed with authority. "I think yaw a bit outnumbered tonight."

"That's a'ight, it won't be the first time, damn sure won't be the last." Remy smiled an evil smile at Kane and pretended to wipe the red dot away from his chest as if he were brushing away lint. The infrared beam continued its treacherous dance across the man's chest.

"Oh, it will be the last—don't get that shit twisted—if you don't do what the fuck I just said, and do it right the fuck now!" Kane's crew was getting antsy, and though Kane would not have had a problem offing both men right there, he knew that was not the way Ray wanted it done.

The seconds seemed to drone on as the two groups of men stood there with their guns drawn, no one wanting to give in to the other.

"So make a fuckin' move den," Kane said.

After considering the explosiveness of the situation, Remy, the older, more experienced of the men, made a decision. "Listen, you tell Ray we want to continue doing business with him. The shit he's selling is top-notch and for right now, we will continue to do business." With a nod, Remy motioned for his boy to put his gun away. He slowly complied with a smirk and a twist of his lips, sliding his gun into the holster on his hip.

Kane glanced over and nodded to his boys to secure their weapons. They followed instructions, making their guns disappear inside the top of their sagging, baggy

K. Roland Williams

jeans.

"Yeah, I'll pass the fuckin' message along." Kane sneered and took a few steps back.

Business complete, both groups of men backed away to their vehicles. The Lexus backed out from the rear of the club, passed the security post and went into the street. The bright halogens of the convertible were eventually overcome by the darkness of night, and the small car was swallowed up by it.

"See how it's done, fellas? Quick and easy. If Ray would have let me do this shit where we usually do it, you two would be burying their country asses right now in a lime pit in the deep woods. We'd be one hundred G's richer, and we would *still* be up five keys of coke. Ray's ass is slipping. Getting old, I guess."

The two youngins looked at each other, trying to absorb the game and learn how to make a deal go through without getting killed in the process. They had lucked out tonight; no guns had been shot, no bodies would be buried.

"A'ight, let's bounce out." Kane eyed the bag of money and wondered if Raymond would break him off a little extra taste for his hard work this time. Ray had gotten selfish and greedy lately, and Kane refused to be a low-level street lieutenant forever. Something would have to give. Ray was clearly trying to get out of the business, Kane thought, trying to get a few more big paydays, maybe before retirement. Probably invest in the

K. Roland Williams

music industry following the dirty-ass footprints of Vic Sweet. That's why he'd been so sloppy lately; his heart wasn't in the game no more.

Well, that was fine with Kane. He would be more than happy to take over the business and run it the way he saw fit. They were moving way too much weight now with the corner spots and the crack houses that Kane set up and managed. Money was starting to flow again, and Kane wanted his fuckin' share of the loot. He thought to himself, *Shit, I got to eat, too.*

K. Roland Williams

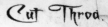
three

Quincy returned from the bathroom and was sitting back at the bar, pondering Neecy's line of questioning a few minutes before as she strolled back over with another drink. This time it was in a champagne flute and filled carefully to the top. He gave the girl a curious look and took the glass from her hand.

"What's up, baby girl? You know I'm drinking vodka tonight, not champagne."

"Tell that to Miss Thang over there across the bar, it came from her."

Neecy twisted her lips and huffed in what Quincy discerned as jealousy, motioning her head in the direction of the woman who sent the drink.

Quincy turned to look at the source of Neecy's concern. The woman looked vaguely familiar to Quincy, but he couldn't quite place her face. He knew most of the regulars on a first-name basis, and he certainly would not have forgotten this dime piece.

K. Roland Williams

She sat regally across the bar, a vision wrapped in Prada. Quincy took notice that it may have been the neon-lit bar, but the woman seemed to radiate light. Her slim cocoa frame was layered in tiers of black silk and cinched in gray satin, her large eyes luminous. She was flawless, and from across the L-shaped bar, she was fine as hell, a Gabrielle Union kind of fine—tall, elegant and classy. Her hair was meticulously styled, and it softly caressed the curves of her gently sculpted shoulders. She looked like money had been an old friend to her, and if she came from new money, she was washed in lots of it.

The woman stood up and smiled, raising her glass to toast Quincy. Seductively taking a sip of the bubbling champagne, she lowered her glass with a look in her eye that hinted at something more than just a simple toast. Her tennis bracelet caught the light and sparkled.

Watching the woman and then looking back at Q, Neecy apprehensively walked away to get back to work, thinking that maybe she should keep an eye on him.

The stranger licked away the droplets of the champagne from her lips with a slow sweep of her tongue and gave Q a seductive gaze, motioning for him to come to her. Quincy had forgotten Neecy for a moment. Shit, they had gone out a few times but they weren't an item or anything, not yet. Q tried his best to convince himself of this. It was true that Q respected Neecy's good-girl persona; nevertheless, this woman across the bar called to

K. Roland Williams

him. There was something behind her eyes and the sexy gloss on her lips that piqued his curiosity and made his dick jump inside his Calvin Klein briefs. That instant chemistry was a motherfucker, and Q was caught up in its power.

The dance floor was packed. The music was loud and rhythmic, and the club pulsed to the tempo of a sequence of high-pitched R. Kelly riffs and Jeezy lyrics. *"Go Getta"* was bangin' the speakers out.

Before Quincy took a step toward the woman, Kane appeared out of nowhere, flanked by his two young thugs. "Ray wants to have a word with you," he said dryly. His thick gold Cuban link chain and diamond medallion twinkled under the club's psychedelic light show. He held a stuffed Pacers duffle bag in his hand. A cluster of thin scars on his forehead interrupted his perfectly trimmed hairline, and the permanent scowl on his face wrinkled his brow.

"Give me a minute, Kane," Quincy said to him with a frown.

"You don't have a minute ... Quincy."

"Whatever, bruh." Quincy looked up to the second-floor window, where Ray's office was positioned above the dance floor of the club. Ray had a bird's eye view of everything that went on in his establishment. He rarely left his sanctuary and could often be seen up there gloating in his success with a drink and cigar in hand.

He stood statuesquely in the window, glaring down

K. Roland Williams

on the club through the etched frosted glass, gesturing for Quincy to come up to his office—an invitation that did not come very often. The woman who had motioned to Quincy distracted Ray as well. He was clearly focused on her. *Out of everyone in here, why her?* Quincy thought.

Quincy would go to Ray's office eventually, but his first priority was to go over and find out a little more about that fine-ass woman who sent the drink so that he could properly thank her, officially introduce himself and get her phone number—exactly in that order.

Kane seemed to notice the woman also. He did a double take when he saw her, and his eyes narrowed. Kane locked gazes with her and shot her an intimidating look. She looked back to the room above, where Ray stood watching.

Quincy noted the interaction between the three, and he looked back up at Ray. For a brief second he thought he saw just the slightest hint of a smile on Ray's face. When Quincy looked back where the mysterious woman had been sitting just moments before, all that remained was the half-empty glass she had just toasted with, an impression of gold lip gloss still visible on the side of the flute.

Quincy scanned the crowded dance floor back to the rear of the club where the V.I.P. room was situated. The red velvet rope was still in place and a huge security guard blocked the entry to the room like a line backer. The woman was nowhere to be seen. As quickly as she

K. Roland Williams

had appeared, she had disappeared. "Oh well," he said, disheartened, "I guess it just wasn't meant to be, not tonight anyway."

At that moment, the girl from earlier, Valerie, walked over to Q and tapped him on his shoulder, buzzed like hell and whispering. "So what's up, baby? You gonna let me get some of that dick or what? It's almost last call and I'm horny as hell!"

"Look, sweetie, I can't do it right now. I got some other shit to attend to." Q looked up at Ray's window. He was gone.

"Well, you have my number," she said, disappointed. "Give me a call sometime."

"Yeah ... rain check."

Quincy glanced over at Neecy, but he already knew what to expect. She looked at him and shook her head in disappointment. Quincy felt bad for a few seconds, but the playa in him wouldn't allow him to sulk too much. He had to keep it movin' and Raymond was waiting.

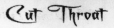
four

Maneuvering up the curved, semi-circular stairwell, Quincy followed it into the second-floor bar area, passing a couple along the stairs sipping cognac and making plans to take the evening to the next level.

The second floor of The Melody Room was as crowded as the first, but the vibe upstairs had more of a trendy lounge feel. The single large room was expensively decorated and broken up into several smaller sitting areas where couples and singles sat in groups that were more intimate, conversing, drinking and laughing. Raymond spared no expense on the club; everything was top shelf, and it showed.

Reluctantly, Quincy left the comfort of the crowded room and followed the long, dark, narrow corridor leading into Raymond's office. He could feel the anxiety building up in his gut; his palms were sweaty and his pulse raced like a Quarter horse out of the gate. Quincy had no reason to feel nervous about anything, but

K. Roland Williams

Raymond's unpredictable personality, reputation and scary demeanor let you know that you were never allowed to get comfortable around him. He preferred that everyone who had a reason to be in his presence did so uncomfortably.

The door to Raymond's office was covered in a gaudy gold metal leaf with a custom plaque above it that read *Head Nigga in Charge* in bright red block letters. Quincy knocked, waited and then entered the office. Raymond was back at the window. His broad back stretched the fabric of the hand-made, three-thousand-dollar Italian suit jacket to its extreme.

The room was cold and smelled of cigars, Pine-Sol and liquor.

"Close the door and have a seat." Raymond James' rumbling voice resembled ungreased gears of machinery.

Raymond was a big man who looked liked he could have played pro football in his younger days. His shoulders and back were wide and his chest was stout. He had the features of a true African: blue-black shiny skin, with a face that looked like it was sculpted from black marble. His eyes and teeth were in stark contrast against that skin, and Raymond did not apologize for it. In fact his appearance had always worked to his advantage—maybe not with the women, but the men were always intimidated by his stature and looks. He always seemed to get his way even as a young man. No one ever had the balls to tell him no.

He lowered his large frame down into the plush leather chair that sat behind the meticulously polished mahogany desk. If he was nothing else, he was neat. The chair's springs groaned in response to the load.

"Can I offer you anything, Quincy ... a drink?" Ray's thick, dark lips split apart, exposing a gold tooth amidst a sea of white, his bald head shining in the overhead light.

"No thanks, Ray. I'm good."

"Is that right? Good, huh?"

Raymond reached into a wooden humidor, pulling out a Cuban cigar, and snipped the end with a gold monogrammed cutter. As he snipped the cigar, the diamonds on his pinky ring caught the light as the cigar's stub toppled to the desk below.

"If you knew what I had to pay to get these fuckin' things ... fuckin' Cuban-U.S. embargo. Suit yourself." Raymond lit the cigar and took several shallow pulls on the stogy until the tip burned bright red. Thick smoke began to plume upwards, framing his huge, round face.

"You wanted to see me?" Quincy asked.

"Yeah, I wanted to talk to you about a few things." Ray shifted in the seat next to a picture of himself and Bernie Mac smiling, both with cigars in their mouths.

"Quincy, I've got to tell you that I was a little skeptical in the beginning about letting you cats come in here and play, that new sound of yours wasn't what southeast

K. Roland Williams

brothas was used to grooving to, you know I'm old school. However, you *did* say you could bring a younger, more professional crowd through the doors with that professional dough to spend, and here we are almost two years later and the crowds haven't stopped yet." Ray reached into his pocket, pulled out a handkerchief and dabbed the beads of sweat from his brow.

"I don't want you to think that I haven't noticed. In fact, I appreciate it so much that I want to make you another offer, an offer that I think you will like."

"You have my attention," Quincy said, searching the man's hollow black eyes.

"Well, I know the contract that we have is a loose one to say the least, and you aren't making the dough that you should be making. I want to give you a bump up, let's say two hundred more a weekend to start." Raymond stood up and removed his suit jacket and released the top few buttons of his flamboyant black and gold Versace shirt, his thick neck now exposed, displaying the infamous wide scar that traversed from one side of his throat to the other. A few inches deeper and Ray may have found himself separated from his head.

The large pistol in his shoulder holster was now showing as well. Quincy found that he was inadvertently staring at the scar on the man's neck, drawn to it like a moth to a flame. He had to make himself look away and into the man's dark, abysmal eyes, better those eyes than the scar. Everyone knew not to talk about or even

K. Roland Williams

look at the scar—it was forbidden.

"So you want to give the band and me a raise, you want to give all of us more money?" Quincy, shaken up by the man's offer, had not heard him correctly.

"No, I said I want to give *you* a raise. If I meant the band, I would have said *the band*."

Raymond stood and walked over to the bar and poured himself a shot of cognac which he threw back hard, the scar on his throat quivering with the up and down movement of his ruined Adam's apple. Quincy could see that the real Raymond James was there in front of him now, in all of his gangster glory, the Raymond who had the reputation for doing dirty business and murdering niggaz to make deals go his way. Quincy wondered if Ray would pull the gun from its holster on him to drive his point across.

Quincy took a few brief moments to consider the offer, stroking his mustache as he did when in deep thought. Perspiration accumulated on his forehead despite the room's cool temperature, and the light linen outfit suddenly felt heavier and thicker than it should; it felt like armor. Quincy tried to prepare himself for the drama that he knew was inevitable. He responded with a very calm and level voice. "Ray, I appreciate the offer, but you know I can't accept any more money without the guys getting more cheddar, too. That shit won't fly with them, I—"

Ray cut him off in mid-sentence, "It wasn't a problem

K. Roland Williams

six months ago when you came to me for that little talk about your money situation when you needed to get the apartment. You even offered to work it out doing other things for me. I gave you another few hundred a week plus the two grand advance, which you're still paying back by the way ... the band was unaware of *that* little incident, were they not? Besides, I know how much you crave that fuckin' attention on the stage. I think you need to start thinking about a solo career anyway."

"A solo career?"

The door to the office squeaked open slowly, allowing the music of the club to meander its way inside the room. It was quickly muffled as Kane shut the door and came up behind Quincy, as if telepathically cued by Ray. Kane threw Ray a duffle bag and gave him a nod. No words were exchanged between the two men. Ray slid the bag behind his desk and out of sight.

"Listen, Quincy, here's how it's gonna play out. You *are* going to re-up with me, and we *are* going to do a little ... renegotiation." Ray's voice was more of a whisper now. His jaw was tight as he spoke, and he narrowed his eyes to coal black slits.

"I been talking to a few of my connects downtown, and I've made some arrangements to put you in the studio with a well-known local producer. In the meantime, you will still work here on Friday and Saturday nights singing lead with the band like you've been doing. Trust me, this is your time right now, and we both gonna get paid in the process. Don't worry, all the upfront costs come out of my pocket, and we may even pull in your boys from time to time to play on some of the background tracks."

"Yeah, those are called recoupable fees, and I'll have to pay for everything eventually out of my end; I know how it works, Ray, better than you." Quincy had mixed feelings about Ray's slanted proposition. The idea of having a real record deal made Q's dick hard. The music was all that Q cared about, but the price, Q was sure, would be more than he was willing to pay. Doing business with Ray would be like signing a pact with the devil, and he knew it.

Slightly amused, Ray leaned down and reached slowly into his desk drawer, still chewing on the Cuban cigar. Quincy held his ground but watched Ray's hand as he withdrew it from the desk.

"Oh by the way, Ray, it *was* Miss you-know-who at the bar just now. She sent this nigga a drink, too ... a glass of Moët," Kane interjected, trying to instigate Ray's anger with Quincy.

"Hmmm, I wonder what the fuck she was doing here at my spot. Her backstabbing ass got a whole lot of nerve up in here as if she got a free pass. She need to carry her ass back to Victor where she belongs."

"Give me the word, Ray, and I can make *all* that shit go away!"

"Naw, not yet, Kane. The cops still would come right

K. Roland Williams

to my ass if anything happened to Victor. When the time is right, we will collect all debts, little nephew. For now, keep your mouth shut and your eyes open."

Disappointed with Ray's response, Kane nudged Quincy's shoulder.

Quincy swung around in response to the nudge, ready to swing on Kane, fed up with his constant bull-shit.

"Yo, nigga, I told you once before about touching me!" Quincy puffed up.

Before Quincy knew it, Kane's nine millimeter was halfway out of its holster. Quincy could see the dull black metal of the weapon under his suit jacket, and half a blur later the cold steel was pressed hard against Quincy's right temple. The safety was off. He'd heard the metallic clicking of the hammer cocking back into place. Quincy's heart was pounding at full speed, and Kane was close enough to his face that he could smell the Heineken on his hot, panting breath.

"Leave the gangsta shit to the gangstas, pretty boy. Just sign the fuckin' contract and everythang will be over, you can go back to focusing on singin' to the bitch-es. That is what *you* do, ain't it?" Kane smirked hard. He was in his element amidst the tough talk and adrenaline rush that went along with the violence.

Quincy had underestimated the thug as just talk. He would not underestimate Kane a second time.

Kane looked over at Ray, silently requesting permission to squeeze the trigger. However, Raymond was lost in thought, transfixed with memories of Antoinette and the times that they had shared before the war raged between him and Victor. Still awaiting Raymond's response, Kane called out to his uncle to snap out of his trance.

Quincy knew that his singing was one of Ray's main sources of income. He was not about to allow Kane to do shit, but it didn't change the fact that he still had a fuckin' gun to his head for the first time ever in his life. He quickly started to doubt his importance to Raymond and question why he was working at the club to begin with.

Kane slowly pulled back on the trigger. Before Quincy could move, the hammer slammed down hard with a loud metallic crack. Quincy squeezed his eyes together in response to the horrific sound. The gun, however, was empty; there was no flash and no loud pop, just uneasy, roaring silence.

Breaking the quiet, Kane immediately busted out into laughter as he pushed Quincy back hard against the desk. Kane removed a full clip from his jacket pocket and inserted it into the handle of the weapon. He slid the action back and a live hollow point mechanically fed itself into the gun's hungry receiver.

Without a word, Ray held his palm up for Kane to stop the game; his point had been made abundantly clear, and Ray didn't want any accidents with his

K. Roland Williams

nephew's itchy-ass trigger finger being what it was.

Kane was an obedient dog, so he bit his lip and slid the weapon reluctantly back into its holster.

"I knew I liked you for a reason, you got heart, nigga ... for a club singa." Ray smiled, his gold tooth sparkling in the overhead track lights. He pulled out a stack of papers from the desk drawer and thumped it down hard onto the desktop. A black and gold Montblanc followed from the same drawer. It was a contract.

"Sign," was the sole word from the killer turned nightclub owner.

So this is what the devil looks like? Quincy thought to himself. He was still shaking from the ghetto round of Russian roulette, and he tried to steady himself and drum up the courage to flat out say, "Fuck no!" He never quite got the words to form on his lips.

"Oh, so what, I can't even read it?" Quincy asked, trying not to sound too shaken.

"What, you don't trust me?" Raymond asked sarcastically with a smile.

"What is that, some kind of trick question?" Quincy said with an angrier tone, his heart pounding to the rhythm of the upbeat number playing in the club.

"Nigga, you can read it, *after* you sign it," Kane added.

Quincy hesitated for a second and Kane walked back up on him, the nine millimeter making its second appearance of the night.

"Yo, nigga, play time is over and Nina loaded for real

K. Roland Williams

now. Don't make me *really* put it on yo' black ass."

"Yeah, well, it's easy to be tough when you the only one wit' one, nigga."

"Well, it ain't my fault you only brought your looks to a gun fight, pretty boy. Next time come strapped," Kane said with a twisted look on his face, pissed that Q was talking back to him, disrespecting.

Quincy locked eyes with Ray, the instincts of survival welling up inside of him. It took everything that he had not to go across the desk at Ray's ass. He might have had a fair chance with the out-of-shape gangster if it weren't for that wily nigga behind him with the gun. Quincy tried to remember that he was a singer and why he was there to begin with, but he was no punk; he had been raised in the Capitol Heights projects on the gritty streets of the northeast side of Washington, D.C. However, he knew when he was outgunned.

Kane smiled as Quincy slowly and apprehensively signed the crooked contract. "Good boy," Raymond said.

Quincy fantasized about grabbing a knife and reopening the scar on Raymond's bloated, sweaty throat, finishing the job that another man started.

"Fuck both of you. This shit ain't over," Quincy said, aloud this time, not giving a fuck.

"Your ass really belongs to me now, for another five years. After that, you can do whatever the fuck you want. Don't worry, I have plans for you in the studio. You'll get your chance at the big time, but I'll get a piece

K. Roland Williams

of that record industry dough I keep hearing so much about. Shit, if Diddy can do it, so can I."

After Quincy had spent almost two years at the club without any major problems, Ray's devilish ass finally showed his true colors. Quincy had known that it would only be a matter of time—things had been too quiet, had gone too fuckin' well.

Quincy tried to move his feet away from the spot on the floor, but they felt as if they had been concreted down. They would not budge without a jackhammer or dynamite. He just stood there for a few seconds, staring at the contract on the table, dazed and pissed.

Kane mouthed under his breath, "Your ass is mine," as he poured himself a drink. Raymond stood there amidst the haze of the cigar smoke and tension in the room, while the club music reverberated against the walls and rumbled the glass in the office window.

Ray walked over and peered through the blinds. He allowed the adrenaline of the power rush and effects of the liquor to travel through his blood stream like dope as he looked out over his night club, satisfied with the crowded dance floor, bar and tables. *It will be a good tally tonight,* he thought, *it will be a damn good night indeed.* Ray looked over his left shoulder. "Now get the fuck out of my office before I really lose my mothafuckin' patience. Kick rocks, nigga, and leave the signature page. Don't forget to read over the contract. I don't want you to feel like I cheated you or no shit."

K. Roland Williams

five

The bright flash and loud bang of the thirty-eight snub nose pointed at Quincy's skull startled him out of the nightmare. He was sure that he could still smell the pungent odor of the gun smoke and was elated to see clean sheets and a blood-free white wall next to his bed once he was able to crack his hazy eyes apart.

Q hauled himself out from under the sweat-soaked sheets, rubbing his temple with a trembling hand. It wasn't Kane who had just shot him in the dome, but a woman in the shadows, whose face he couldn't quite make out.

"Fuck, those things are too damn real." Q dry washed his face with both hands and tried to shake the thought of the dark shadow that just smoked him in the nightmare. The sun lazily crept through the slits of his dusty blinds, flooding the small bedroom of his apartment with the crimsons and burnt oranges of early morning. The next-door neighbor's television blared gospel music

K. Roland Williams

through the wall above his black leather headboard. It would appear that the Thomas household was having their Sunday morning couch ministry right on schedule, and Bishop T.D. Jakes was on fire.

Quincy looked over at the digital clock. The large blue numbers read 7:32, and the pang in his empty stomach demanded immediate attention. The ceiling fan still rotated and hummed sluggishly overhead, washing his naked, athletic frame with warm air as he tried to clear his head and wipe away the cobwebs and confusion of the chain of events from the night before. He still couldn't believe what happened last night. It had all been so surreal.

Quincy's long legs whipped around the side of the queen-sized bed. He wiped the sweat from his forehead, sleep from his eyes and ran his fingers through his damp, curly black mane, wishing that he had invested in the small air conditioner that he priced at Wal-Mart weeks before. The thought that he had to go to rehearsal tonight and tell the band the news of the contract quickly replaced his need to eat with nausea.

He still had not even read a single page of the contract. The law did not take extortion lightly, but Quincy had to find another way to figure out how to get out of this mess. He didn't need this type of thing to complicate his one purpose for being at the club in the first place. That would be the quickest way to end up on Ray's shit list and in a body bag.

K. Roland Williams

The document was still on the small wooden side table where he had thrown it the night before. He prayed that a miracle might make the damn thing disappear into the black abyss of night, but he had no such luck—it still sat there in its hundred-something page glory, mocking him.

"Something's got to give. I have to figure this shit out."

Almost on cue, the phone rang, startling Quincy out of his contemplation. He stood on unsteady feet as the cold tiled floor rose up to greet him as the only thing in the apartment that wasn't one hundred degrees. He grabbed the cordless receiver from its place on the cradle.

"Hello." The voice on the other end didn't wait for Q to give a greeting. The woman's voice was not a familiar one, but it was very sexy and commanded Quincy's attention.

"Hello, did I wake you?" the woman's tone was warm and hospitable for so early in the morning.

"No, I'm up … who's this?"

"Sorry to call you so early. You don't know me, but I was the one at the club last night who sent you the Moët. You sounded great by the way. You and the band have a very unique sound, a style that I haven't heard before."

Quincy perked up. Any sleep that clouded his head was quickly washed away that very instant.

"Thanks, I appreciate the compliment. We've worked

K. Roland Williams

very hard to develop our own sound. Just out of curiosity, how did you get my number?"

"Let's just say that I am a very resourceful woman; I have my ways."

"I don't doubt that. I'm only asking because before you disappeared last night I had planned on coming over and thanking you for the champagne, but you left in such a rush, I never had a chance to."

Quincy remembered Kane's comment to Ray the night before about the woman sending him the drink. It perplexed Quincy, but he figured he would keep it to himself for now.

"Umm, something came up." Her voice went from extremely sexy to very business-like in a fraction of a second, changing the subject and transitioning into her business spiel.

"My name is Antoinette Sweet, and I represent Cut Throat Records. You may have heard of us?"

"Yeah, I've heard of Cut Throat Records. You're one of the largest black-owned Hip Hop labels on the East Coast."

Quincy tried to stay cool, calm and collected. It appeared that opportunity had knocked again, or more accurately, called his home number directly.

"Listen, I'll get right to the point," the woman said. "I have the authority to make you an offer."

Quincy had been given his share of propositions in the last two days, but this offer couldn't be much worse

than Ray's contract, so he indulged the woman.

"What do you have in mind?" His curiosity tugged hard at him.

"I specifically came to the club last night to hear you play ... kind of like a talent scout, if you will. I am part owner and acting A&R director of Cut Throat Records. We are putting our new R&B division into effect to complement the existing Hip Hop division, and I would like to give you an opportunity to become the second R&B act of the label, if things work out, that is. It will be an opportunity to get out of that *hole* that you've been singing in, and put you in the studio ... give you a chance to make some real music—and let the world hear what you can really do. How does that sound?" Antoinette had her sales voice in top gear now and sounded confident that Quincy would take her up on her offer.

Quincy was definitely feeling a little overwhelmed with his overnight success, so he hesitated and decided to play it out a while. He wanted to see where the conversation was headed and where he fit into the equation. Raymond's face still tore through his head like a hurricane. The ragged scar on Ray's throat flashed in Quincy's mind like a bolt of hot white lightning.

Things slowly started to make a little more sense to Quincy. Antoinette Sweet, Victor Sweet and Raymond James were connected. There was definitely a connection—and the more Q ran the conversation that Ray and Kane had the night before through his head, the more he

K. Roland Williams

started to think that they were all tied together through blood.

"Well, all of that sounds good, but I am doing all right at The Melody Room, and Ray has been ... taking good care of me."

He thought about spending years as a slave to Ray's ass, not to mention taking all kinds of shit from that punk-ass nigga, Kane. It just wasn't Quincy's style to go out like that, and it would eventually come down to someone being killed. Quincy figured the odds were not on his side. He subconsciously rubbed his right temple, the spot where Kane's gun had been pressed just a few hours ago. He grimaced at the thought of the barrel of the gun touching his skin.

On the other hand, there was Antoinette, and though under normal circumstances, this would be a dream come true for Quincy and the band, something just wasn't sitting right with this whole thing. It smelled like a set up.

Quincy's momma had taught him long ago, before she passed away and left him alone in the world, that just because something came in a pretty package didn't necessarily make it a good thing.

"Look, Quincy, I called you to see if you would be interested in attending a record release party that we're giving tonight for Cut Throat's latest act, Desiree. If you come out tonight, we can talk a bit more about you possibly coming on board, and what we can offer you as

K. Roland Williams

one of our artists. You would have the backing and resources of a major label with major distribution in several markets in the states and abroad."

"That's where I've seen you before. You're married to the owner of Cut Throat, Victor Sweet. I saw you on the cover of *Essence* magazine a few months ago. Yes, Mrs. Sweet, I'll be there." Quincy tried not to sound excited about the idea of meeting real record label executives, but was doing a poor job of it.

"Good, I will send a car for you at let's say ... 8 p.m., and be on time. By the way, Quincy, you can call me Toni ... let's drop the Mrs. Sweet thing right now."

"Okay, Toni, I'll be there tonight."

"Is there another name *you* want to go by? I'm not sure Quincy is quite right for you ... not as one of my artists anyway."

"What do you mean? That's the name my momma gave me and the name that's on my birth certificate," he said with a laugh. "My peoples call me Q for short. You can, too, if you like."

"Q sounds all right, we'll have to see about that though. See you tonight ... Q."

The phone call ended as abruptly as the brief meeting the night before at the club. The beautiful black woman, with whom Quincy had not officially met, hung up on him before they really could have a full conversation.

"This shit is getting stranger by the minute." It was as

K. Roland Williams

if he stepped into a crazy episode of *"The Twilight Zone,"* but in the hood. Raymond's contract sat staring at Quincy on the side table as if it was eavesdropping. He picked up the heavy stack of legal verbiage and dropped it back down hard on the table again. "Fuck you, Ray. Take your contract and shove it up your fat black ass!"

He would have time to deal with that shit soon enough, but right now he wanted to savor the phone call from the first lady of Cut Throat Records. He lay his brown frame back down on his bed, still butt-ass naked, and cursed the warm rush of air that he was getting from the wobbly ceiling fan. His life was spinning a lot like the fan. The question was, how would things end?

For now he would play the game out, bide his time and let the fuckin' cards land where they may.

six

"What do you think, Toni?" Victor Sweet yelled across the cavernous room of the penthouse and the music that played over the wall-mounted Bang & Olufsen CD player.

The song that played was by the latest Cut Throat Records artist, Desiree. Her low vibrato danced and slid easily in and out of the mid tempo track.

Antoinette carefully contemplated the offer she had just made the nightclub singer on the phone moments before, ignoring her husband's question.

Quincy was truly a talented singer, and had the look and swagger that could propel him into stardom. His tall, athletic body, perfect smile, great looks and sun-kissed skin would be magical in front of the cameras. She thoughtfully considered the possibilities with the young crooner and twisted a lock of her hair tightly with her fingers until it curled and spun itself loose. She smiled at the endless possibilities.

K. Roland Williams

"Damn, she sounds good, don't she?" Victor left the shower still naked, leaving a trail of water across the bamboo floor, air drying and snapping his fingers as he walked, his penis swaying side to side with each damp step.

Antoinette responded to his question with a roll of her eyes and a huff.

"I asked you what you thought about this song." Vic wrapped his large, muscular arms around his wife's petite shoulders and squeezed her tightly.

"It's no hit," she replied dryly.

"What do you know about a hit?" Victor snapped. "You'll see what kind of talent she has when those record sales start rolling in. You know I wrote this song myself? *We get all of the publishing.*" He sang the words melodically like an excited child.

"Whatever you say, Vic, whatever you say." Antoinette was sarcastic with her tone of voice and didn't seem to care about the consequences of her disdain; as far as she was concerned, their marriage was far beyond caring at this point.

"I have some ... *business* to attend to later. I should be done wrapping it up right before the party tonight."

She cut her eyes sharply at her husband's reflection in the mirror. She allowed them to roam his face, searching for a hint of the lie she was confident he was now telling.

"Wait a minute, don't tell me that you're still mad

K. Roland Williams

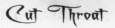
about the other night. I told you that I didn't come home because I was taking care of *business*. I was wrapping up Desiree's last single. What, let me guess ... that's not good enough for you?"

"Whatever, Vic. I called the studio and Cam said you had just stepped out for a second. You do what you have to do, take care of *your* business, and I'll take care of mine. I just hope that bitch is worth it." She continued brushing her silky, black shoulder-length hair with her sterling silver brush.

"Haven't I given you everything you ever wanted? You have a brand new Benz, a closet full of furs and more ice in your jewelry than a rapper who just got his signing bonus. Not to mention, more money than you could ever spend in a lifetime. When I met you, you were stuck with that fat-ass nigga, hustling on the street, living part-time with your mother until I came and took you away from that life."

Victor didn't appear mad enough to try to hit his wife *this* time, so she pushed his buttons and ignored him.

"Toni, I'm talking to you."

She knew he only called her *Toni* when he was trying to get on her good side. She used to think it was cute. She shifted uncomfortably in her seat, still brushing her hair as Vic gazed at her. His eyes were two smoldering black coals rammed deep into their sockets. His eyes stalking her like a lion stalks a gazelle right before it pounces; something shifted in those eyes of his, and

Toni sensed it.

She resisted him slightly as he reached down and lifted her up to her full five-foot eight-inch height. She had the sterling silver brush ready to jab him in the throat, but instead of hitting her this time, he turned her half-naked body around toward his own. His powerful grip was like steel and his thick biceps flexed with his every movement.

"Look, Toni, I know things have been fucked up lately, but they'll get better, I promise. It takes dedication to build an empire. None of this shit is free—you know that."

His voice was almost convincing. Antoinette noted that her husband had become quite the effective liar over the last few years. Even though he had put her through hell, she still wanted to believe his words, and she felt like shit because of it. And damn, no matter how she tried to cut it, he still looked good as hell.

He slowly brushed away the spaghetti strap that clung to her shoulder, sending her red silk negligee gently to the floor. Victor caressed his wife's ample breasts, licking around the red double cherry tattoo that sat just above her left nipple. He then took her nipple into his hot mouth, sucking deeply. She closed her eyes tightly and allowed herself to picture the young singer with *his* mouth roaming her body. Clenching her fist behind his back, she cursed her nipple's reaction to his warm mouth and lapping tongue while her nipples hardened

K. Roland Williams

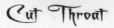

and tingled, sending involuntary signals to the region below.

She opened her eyes long enough to glance down at her own face reflected in the mirror. This was not the life she had fought so hard to get. There had been more to it in the beginning; plans had been made, crimes had been committed, secrets shared, vows and promises broken. Once upon a time, pleasing Vic had been the only thing that she lived for. She would have died or killed for that nigga, but these days—after the money, houses, cars and all the video bitches and model hoes—things were not the same.

He kissed her neck and lowered her body to the soft Persian rug below them. Still damp from his shower, he spread her long, thick thighs apart. She could feel that he was fully erect; the hot spongy flesh of his dick pulsated hard against her thigh. He slid down her body gently kissing as he went. Slowly he rolled his tongue around her clit in small circles, then side to side, taking the sensitive swelling bud into his hungry mouth, sucking in the moist folds of her labia.

He placed his hard dick up against her now-damp opening and pierced her abruptly, abrasively, and began to thrust. Her legs were jack-knifed high up into the air. He moved with the rhythm of his new female artist who now sang a slow melody in the other room, and Antoinette lay on the floor under her husband's weight, wondering if he had fucked Desiree to this very same

K. Roland Williams

song, maybe in the studio on that floor, by the mixing board and sound booth.

Toni succumbed to her husband's desire and allowed herself to drop her guard for the moment. Why not use him as he had used her so many times in their rocky past? She moaned for what seemed like an eternity and came, and with his last selfish, frenzied thrust, he exploded inside of her. His shoulders hunched and his body tensed like metal cable, then immediately went limp.

Victor laid his entire weight on his wife's slim frame so that she could barely breathe before he rolled off to one side and slid out of her, his hot thick cum slowly oozing out of her as well. The room whirled around her as she contemplated the meeting with the new young singer, Quincy, Vic's huge insurance policy, the multi-million-dollar record label that she helped build and how she would make all of it hers, to do with as she pleased. Everything was falling into place so far. A few more pieces to go ... and the puzzle would be complete.

K. Roland Williams

seven

Detective Jack Renaldy leaned back in his hard wooden chair and scrutinized the large corkboard hanging on the wall with feverish anticipation. His Beretta nine millimeter was squeezed tightly into his shoulder holster and it ached against his ribs. The loud metal fan hummed and rotated side to side, pushing hot, musty air around the small, dimly lit room.

His icy blue eyes were the only hint of color in the gray box that doubled as his office, and they tightened to thin slits as he scrutinized an individual photo that sat dead center on his perp board. He had convinced himself that he didn't need the glasses that sat no more than three feet away from him on his desk, next to his daughter Emily's high school graduation picture, but his eyes strained nonetheless, and his head began to throb with the monotonous dull ache that he had learned to tolerate.

Renaldy's hands clenched and unclenched, his arthri-

K. Roland Williams

tis doing a number on him as usual. He was having a hard time trying to come up with a feasible plan to get through his dilemma. He couldn't focus for some reason. He scanned the office, noticing that his desk was a hot fucking mess: Starbucks coffee cups overflowed out of the garbage can and onto the drab linoleum floor. The Krispy Kreme doughnut boxes had long been empty but sat piled and forgotten, a heap of calories and a heart attack waiting to happen. He would clean the office soon, just not today. He went on considering his options.

The case board displayed an incomplete hierarchy of pictures. Each photo was given its own place on the uneven tree. The latest major drug war in the Metro D.C. had gotten out of hand. For a solid year, the violence spilled out of the hoods and dangerously close to the nicer parts of town. The politicians had plans for gentrification of the city and refused to have their multi-million-dollar plans ruined by a handful of criminals. The result was the city's officials declaring war on the bad guys. The problem demanded immediate results, and Renaldy was the veteran narcotics detective assigned to the case. Currently without a partner, he worked the case loads solo, which was the way he preferred it.

The detective spun the details of his plan cinematically through his head, dividing the ideas up into manageable sections so as not to overlook anything pertinent. He ran his chubby fingers through his thinning brown hair to no avail. He would have to find a way to get close to a man who had security with him around the clock and more money than Renaldy would ever see in a lifetime.

"I can't even get close to this guy, let alone find a way to whack him."

Renaldy reached into his pocket and tore open a small blue packet, dropped two Alka Seltzer tablets into a warm glass of water and waited while they dissolved, leaving a thin gritty residue that smelled of lemons. He threw the glass back and swallowed the tonic with a gulp followed by a relieving belch of sour air, his ulcers violently reacting to his attempt to get temporary relief from the pain.

In the center of the board sat Renaldy's newest personal assignment and nemesis, the part-time record label CEO and ex-drug dealer Victor Sweet, Renaldy's number one target. Sweet's background read like a true crime novel. He had started his life of crime at the ripe age of fourteen with armed robbery and aggravated assault. A wide variety of felony arrests trailed him into his adult life.

Five years ago, Victor Sweet had saved enough dirty money to invest in studio time for some street thug turned rapper. That endeavor took off and facilitated his rise to fame and semi-legitimate money. It didn't take Victor long to parlay his connection with Ortega, the Columbian crime organization, into bigger and more lucrative things. As far as the law could tell, Victor was

K. Roland Williams

clean and out of the game. He had made enough money to buy his way out. He still hung out with the street element, or the street element still wanted to hang out with him now that he was a star. There was always a kinship between crime and the music business, and Victor had been quite the star in both.

He had become a millionaire many times over by the age of thirty, and showed no signs of slowing down. Neither the local police nor the FBI had been able to indict Victor on any of the crimes of which they suspected him, two of which were murder, before his career change, but Renaldy was working diligently on changing that. He didn't have a choice—Raymond would expect results and soon. The five thousand a month Ray started paying Renaldy for protection, tip offs on busts and rousting the competition would have to be earned if Renaldy wanted to live long enough to see retirement. He would also be adding murder to his list of duties.

On the board underneath Victor Sweet were Raymond James and his nephew, Kane, the police chief's number two priority. Raymond James was also affiliated with the Ortega crime organization. Victor and Raymond had started in the game together as boys slinging nickel and dime bags of weed and then heroin on the corners of B-More and D.C., and that grew into a larger organization when they started moving major weight.

The only evidence against Raymond so far was a few illegal wiretaps that brought up his name as a player in

Ortega's syndicate. The narcotics squad had gotten very close to shutting down Raymond's entire drug operation, but when he was almost murdered a few years back, his dealing seemed to stop altogether. After he recuperated, he brought his nephew on board to assist in running the family business.

Kane was the front man on the street and Ray's right-hand man, lieutenant and enforcer. Narcotics never quite figured out who tried to kill Raymond, as he kept his mouth shut tight—some code of the street bullshit—though Renaldy now knew who would have wanted him dead. The FBI and narcotics department still thought Raymond had some dealings with Ortega, though he went through great lengths to appear clean.

He was the owner of several local nightclubs, titty bars and check cashing stores in the city. The club he owned, The Melody Room, was his biggest source of income, netting him fifty thousand plus a week, and that was just one of his establishments. Raymond was careful to pay his taxes and keep everything on the up and up, so they couldn't get him on tax evasion.

Renaldy looked over his shoulder to make sure no one was close to his door as he quickly removed the pictures of Raymond James and Kane and slid them into a folder that remained unmarked. That folder was sealed with other evidence and placed into Renaldy's top drawer, and the drawer was locked for safekeeping. If all went as planned, after time, Renaldy could ensure that

K. Roland Williams

Raymond disappeared off the case file and hopefully, if Renaldy did his job properly, Raymond would begin to slip off the radar of the police chief's hit list, or at least that was the plan that he sold to Raymond. On the other hand, the hidden evidence could be used as a bartering chip in the event that shit got ugly for the cop. He would use it to try to keep Raymond at bay as a last resort if it came down to that.

Now we're getting somewhere, he thought to himself.

Focusing his attention back on Victor, the cop looked for a flaw in his past, a weak link that might allow him to get close to the man. His eyes roamed past the unfortunate photos of dead black men stretched out, murdered in the streets, some Victor's men and some Raymond's. From D.C. to Baltimore, the streets had run red with blood when Victor was still in the game.

He tried to destroy Raymond and almost accomplished his goal. Victor came close to winning the war, but it took Ortega getting wind of the problem all the way in Columbia and threatening to kill both men and their families if the bloody rampage didn't end. He supplied both men with cocaine, and their war was ruining his business and drawing way too much attention to his organization, but the damage had already been done.

Both Raymond James and Victor Sweet agreed to a cease-fire, at least for the time being. Both men knew that anything less would clearly mean the end for them. Now things were different and both men had seemingly changed their lives.Renaldy knew he had made a pact with the devil, but with his meager cop's pension, which he wouldn't get until he retired in another six years, and his daughter's school tuition, he figured what the hell, he had played it by the book most of his career, why not take a little chunk for himself? Renaldy walked to his door and closed it tight to ensure privacy. He picked up his throw-away cell, flipped it open and dialed a cell phone number.

"Speak on it," the voice growled through the phone.

"Mr. James, that thing we discussed, it's started. I will keep you posted on the investigation and my progress, but I assure you that you have nothing to be concerned about. I have it all under control."

"Well, you better, cop. I don't like surprises, and I'm paying you good money to make sure that I don't have any. We understand each other?"

"Yes, we do, Ray."

"Oh, and by the way, I want that *candy shop* closed and out of the equation for good ... sooner rather than later."

"I was just thinking about that. What are the chances that you can get one of your people to do the wet work and take Victor out? *You people* are much better at it than I could ever be."

"Why are you saying names over an open line?" Raymond paused. Renaldy could hear him breathing in the phone. "Don't you have a daughter who attends

K. Roland Williams

George Mason University?"

Renaldy's back straightened stiff as a board and his hair stood up on his red neck. "There is no fuckin' need to bring my family into this. I will take care of it." Renaldy's eyes involuntarily started to water with the thought of something happening to his only child.

"Well then, I'm glad to see that we understand each other. In the future, when I give you an order, don't ask if I can have someone else handle it. Oh, and for the record, I'll act like I didn't hear that *you people* comment."

The cellular connection was abruptly broken, and Renaldy stood there staring out into space. He snapped out of it, focused in on Victor Sweet's picture, and contemplated the best way to get to him and put him out of commission for good. That would actually satisfy the police chief, the mayor and his greedy constituents. The government would never go after Ortega anyway. He was untouchable, probably even a friend to the U.S. in some twisted capitalistic way.

Besides, Renaldy pondered, taking Victor out would be doing a good deed, a public service. Renaldy tried to convince himself of this.

"Well, maybe this case isn't a total loss after all," he said aloud. "Another nigger off of the street, I might just get a little satisfaction before it's all said and done."

He looked over at the picture of his daughter in her blue and yellow graduation cap and gown. His frown

K. Roland Williams

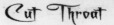

softened and the lines in the corners of his mouth relaxed. "I'm sorry, baby. I guess your mother was right about me after all."

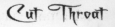

eight

The jet black Mercedes S600 slid gracefully through the city streets. Its metallic skin reflected the quickly passing lights that illuminated the heart of the downtown metropolitan area. The luxury sedan drove down Constitution, passed by the Washington Memorial and eventually purred to a smooth stop alongside the Potomac River outside of the Watergate, infamously historic and prestigious home of Victor and Antoinette Sweet.

The driver slid out of the sedan in his black double-breasted suit and professional driver's cap and opened the rear passenger's door, giving Quincy the celebrity treatment, orders of Antoinette Sweet. The moon was a bright golden ball in the night sky. It was a strange yellow, unlike any Quincy had ever seen, a liquid glow, odd yet beautiful. There was no red carpet waiting, but instead an ocean of overly excited groupies, news media and hopeful artists with demo tapes in hand standing

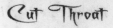

outside of the lobby awaiting the opportunity to get into the party of the month.

The photographers immediately rushed the open car door. Flash bulbs exploded with blinding claps of white light and telephoto lenses focused on Quincy as he exited the car. He was glad he had decided to wear the shades now, despite the fact that it was very dark outside. He felt like a star, and at that very moment, he had an epiphany. There was no doubt in his mind that he would do *whatever* it took to make it finally happen, whatever. Singing at the club was just a taste of what it would really be like, and he wanted more. He craved it desperately like a junkie needed a fix. He jonesed to be a star.

Quincy quickly snapped his ass back to reality as the crowd of photographers and groupies seemed to realize all at once that Quincy was an unknown, not a true celebrity, and went back to focusing on the front door and balcony of the building, hoping to get a glance of the real stars currently inside of the party. The driver pushed through the crowd, motioned to the security camera in the vestibule of the residence and punched a code into the keypad of the security door. The door hummed and the lock magnetically released with a buzz.

"Straight back and to the right, Mr. Underwood. Take this card, slide it into the slot for floor number fourteen. That will take you where you want to go." The driver smiled graciously and turned back to the crowded walk-

K. Roland Williams

way in front of the building.

"Hey, what do I do when I get on the fourteenth floor?"

"Nothing, just walk in. The elevator opens up into the Sweet residence."

The driver smiled again, trying not to embarrass Quincy and point out his lack of experience in the ins and outs of luxury living.

When the elevator reached the top level, it opened onto the marble foyer of the seven-thousand-square-foot apartment that took up the entire fourteenth floor and penthouse of the building. Columns soared up from floor to ceiling, black veined marble seemed to cover every surface and the opulent furniture and decoration was top-notch; not a dollar was spared on the home and it showed.

"Goddamn," Quincy said aloud. His mouth dropped open and his eyes widened to saucers at the sight of the luxurious home. He excitedly lifted a flute of champagne from a serving tray as it passed by, connected to a scantily-clad server whose breasts were barely covered, her nipples perked through her bright red tube top with *Cut Throat* written across the front.

All the important people were at Vic's party. A well-known football player and one of Vic's Hip Hop acts sat and laughed on a leather ultra-contemporary couch, surrounded by a sea of seemingly-fascinated giggling women. Quincy finished his drink and abandoned the glass on a platter while scooping up another glass of champagne.

Posters of Desiree were everywhere, and handouts with her cover art and song playlists were on all the tabletops. The woman herself was there with Vic, being personally introduced to everyone from radio personalities and distribution people to celebrities. Desiree's first single blared over the DJ's system.

Quincy scanned the room curiously, recognizing several faces from commercials, videos and movies. All the A-listers showed up to Victor Sweet's gatherings. Most were too afraid not to, while others knew that by going to Vic's parties they would be seen and considered a part of the in-crowd.

Victor Sweet was working the crowd like a seasoned veteran. He slid in between his guests smiling like a politician, toasting, drinking, greeting and making small talk, but most importantly, promoting his latest up-and-coming act. Victor was tall, handsome, charismatic and most importantly, rich. He was a perfect combination of street thug and successful businessperson. He was a powerful man who was to be respected *and* feared.

Quincy made himself at home, mixing with the crowd. Hopping from each small group of talking people, he gathered his courage and eventually found his way over to Desiree. She was standing by the grand piano, speaking to a tall, thin musician who Quincy recognized from one of his gigs a few years back.

K. Roland Williams

"Earl!" Quincy called out, interrupting the man's conversation with Desiree.

"Quincy Underwood! Small fucking world," the man yelled out, smiling and adjusting his thick glasses on his narrow nose. Slapping Quincy on his shoulder, he said, "How in the hell have you been? Still croonin' to the ladies?" Earl pulled his brim down over his eye and lit a Newport. The cigarette dangled from the corner of his mouth, threatening to fall at any time.

"Have I been singin'? What kind of question is that, old man? I ain't missed a day of singin' something in fifteen years, even if it's 'Happy Birthday.'" Quincy smiled at Desiree, licking his lips and throwing her a hint of his sex appeal and swagger. He was careful to play it off like he wasn't trippin' on her star status.

"Good to see you, man." Checking himself, the man introduced Quincy to Desiree.

"So you're a singer, huh?" she asked, clearly flirting. Her naturally deep voice reminded Q of Toni Braxton.

"Well, I'm no star like you, not yet ... but I do a little somethin', somethin'."

"Well ... *Quincy* was it? Let's see what you can do." Desiree looked Q up and down as if she could eat him up for dinner *and* dessert. Quincy recognized this as an opportunity, and he decided he would take full advantage.

"What do you want me to sing?" Q asked, unafraid of the pressure she was trying to apply.

K. Roland Williams

"Hmmm, let me see ..." she said with a devilish smile. Her long legs were thick and her waist was small, and Q tried not to be caught staring. The diamond belly ring visible under her short shirt sparkled like the canary diamond Cut Throat necklace she wore around her neck. It was clear that Victor Sweet took very good care of his artists. *At least the female artists,* Q thought.

"Let's do a duet together."

"Let's do it," he said. "You got a favorite?"

"As a matter of fact, I do. Do you know *'Nothing Has Ever Felt Like This'* by Will Downing and Rachelle Ferrell?"

"Do I know it? That's one of my favorite duets!" Quincy lied with a straight face and stood next to Desiree as they quickly went over which key they would sing the love song in. A few minutes later they were singing to each other as if they were the only ones in the room.

Victor was puzzled by Quincy. He didn't recognize the man who was uninvited to his party, and as if that weren't enough, he was singing to his jump-off chick—his number two after his wife. But the boy could definitely blow. He had Will's voice down from the high tenor riffs to the low baritone melody. Their voices slid gracefully in and out of the piano's tune like a couple making passionate love together.

The entire party stopped to watch the star and the unknown man sing to each other, and Q ate it up. He

K. Roland Williams

took control as he always did on the stage or in the limelight. He was in his element and the way he reached out
and took Desiree's hand confirmed that he had the kind
of skills that made a woman forget her man and yearn
for just a small sample of Quincy. The women at the
party gathered around and followed every one of Q's
notes as if their lives depended on his voice and body
gyrations.

When Quincy finally saw Antoinette, she was standing at the top of the dramatic sweeping staircase on the
second-floor landing of the penthouse, wearing a sexy-
ass black flowing dress that hugged her waist and
accentuated her hourglass-curved hips. Toni had been
curiously watching the show from the top of the stairs.
She was impressed but not surprised; she had witnessed
Q's skills before, which is why he was there in the first
place.

As Q and Desiree faded the song out with the last
piano chords, all eyes switched to Toni as she scanned
the room and posed like a pro. Desiree kissed Q on the
cheek and whispered something in his ear, then walked
away with a smile as if she had just had the best sex in
her life.

Toni's hair was up, formally pinned in place by an
ivory and gold comb, and her MAC makeup was slight
and applied with perfection. Quincy could see that she
had hosted her share of these parties in the past.

She made a beeline for Quincy. "Glad you could make

K. Roland Williams

it. I see it doesn't take you long to make an impression on the ladies," she said with a smile and a wink, her arms opened wide for a hug. She scanned the guests in the cavernous room, her eyes landing on Victor talking with a woman who had to be over six-foot tall, a model no doubt, one of Victor's favorite choices in a woman. Seeing Vic flirting with the woman motivated Antoinette to do her own flirting.

The DJ played a combination of music, from the latest Cut Throat Records artist who was on the Top Twenty radio playlists, to the latest artist the record label was currently pushing. Vic's right-hand man and partner in crime, Ricky Wright, watched Antoinette from the far side of the room. His eyes roamed her body lustfully. He licked his thick, dark lips as he looked her up and down, careful not to let Victor see the desire in his eyes.

When Antoinette locked eyes with the man, she rolled hers, making it obvious that his staring sickened her. Ricky responded with a wink and a smile from across the room and tipped his glass up sarcastically.

Quincy noticed the signal from Antoinette; clearly there was no love to be found there. "Is everything all right, what was that about?" Quincy asked.

"Oh, he's nobody important, just one of Victor's friends. His job is to do my husband's crap jobs, the ones that Victor won't do, including following me around and keeping an eye on me."

Ricky gave Quincy a belligerent look and turned his

K. Roland Williams

back, continuing to talk with a couch full of half-dressed women.

"You look very nice, and you clean up well," she said, eyeing Quincy's toned body. "I want to thank you for coming. We'll eventually talk again about your future with the label, but tonight, I wanted you to get a chance to see everything from the inside. This could be you in the very near future if you play your cards right and listen to what I tell you."

Quincy kept his cool and tried not to show too much concern or excitement about being so close to his dream.

Victor had his arm around Desiree when he glanced over and saw his wife with Quincy.

Antoinette offered Quincy another drink and then led him by the arm to the balcony that overlooked the city. The glass balcony doors slid open to reveal a gorgeous view of the Potomac River. The moon's reflection danced busily across the still dark water.

"I know you just got here, but what do you think so far?" she asked softly.

"I think I want to see more." Quincy looked deeply into Antoinette's eyes and positioned himself closer to her.

Antoinette's hand brushed against his on the railing and they started to move closer to each other, carefully watching the party and Victor through the glass doors. An Avant tune slowly stirred through the wall of glass

K. Roland Williams

and out onto the penthouse's wide balcony, serenading Quincy and Antoinette.

"We need to meet later, Quincy," Antoinette said, staring out into the distant skyline.

"Later when? Tonight?"

"No, maybe tomorrow we can meet somewhere to discuss your future. You can pick the spot. I will bring some information for you to review, and we can take it from there."

"Why can't we meet at your office?" Quincy looked perplexed.

"I want to have an opportunity to discuss a few things with you in private without my staff all over my shoulder."

"You mean your husband, don't you?" Quincy asked.

At that moment, Victor Sweet came through the double glass doors. Victor's arrival seemed to signal the soothing music to escape over the high balcony and into the city far below them. The sound dissolved with each approaching step the big man took toward Quincy and Toni.

The first thing Quincy noticed was how wide Vic's shoulders were. He was a much larger man in person than he appeared to be on television. He could have played pro football in another life. Quincy slowly retracted his hand from the railing where it rested next to Antoinette's dainty hand.

"So, Toni, who's your friend?" Victor's bravado was

K. Roland Williams

turned on full blast.

"This is Quincy Underwood, the night club singer I went to see perform the other night, who I'd like to try out, erhhh," she quickly recanted, "give an opportunity to."

Victor extended a powerful arm and equally strong hand to shake Quincy's.

"It's a great pleasure to meet you, I've—"

"Can I have a word with my wife please ... Quincy, was it?"

"Yeah, my name is Quincy."

Antoinette, clearly embarrassed by her husband's rudeness, intervened.

"Quincy, why don't you go inside, make yourself comfortable, have a drink and introduce yourself to a few people. I'll find you in a bit, okay?"

"Yeah, Quincy," Victor interjected, "what's mine is yours. Make yo'self at home," he added with a sly smile, still looking into his wife's eyes.

"Sure, I'll be inside." Quincy strolled through the door of the large balcony and back into the party.

"So what's this, you've *all of a sudden* taken a personal interest in the business now and want to suggest acts to me? Since when, Toni?"

"Well, you always wanted me to play more of a part in the business. I figured, why not now? He is a very talented guy."

"I bet he is," Victor added sarcastically. "What makes

you think he's talented enough for my label?"

"Do you remember when I would always give you my input on artists in the beginning? Back then you cared enough about me to take it. Well, I'm giving my input now. Is there a problem with that, Vic?"

"No, no problem, Toni."

"Okay, then I will pursue him as a possible new act and start the paperwork. I'll get with Diana at the office tomorrow morning and start putting together a marketing plan."

"You got it all worked out, I see."

"Yes, I sure do," she replied dryly. "Like I said, he is *very* talented."

"Okay, honey, but one thing—don't get it twisted. I'll be watching."

"I'm sure you will, Victor, I'm sure you will. Or at least Ricky will."

"Oh well, I've got work to do. I'll talk with you later ... oh, and by the way, I'm leaving in a few to—"

"Yeah, I know," Antoinette interrupted, "take care of some business."

"You know me so well." Victor turned and headed back toward the party.

Antoinette smiled to herself as she watched her husband return to Desiree's side. She stood on the balcony, bathing in the bright glow of the full moon, and looked at Quincy standing handsomely in a small group of men, mixing with the crowd. She imagined what it might be

K. Roland Williams

like to fuck Quincy in every room of her husband's multi-million-dollar home.

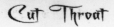
nine

"Damn, I remember playing football in that same field right there where those kids are playing. That was me when I was their age." Raymond reminisced while rubbing the scar on his throat.

Kane looked at his Uncle Ray through the rear-view mirror to where he sat in the back seat of the triple black Range Rover, looking out of a darkly tinted window. The truck's twenty-four-inch DUB rims skipped over pot-holes in Maryland's Oxen Hill neighborhood, the place Ray had grown up, his old stomping ground.

"You know, Kane, when I was a kid running these streets I would never have thought that I would be where I am today ... running the entire fuckin' town. You see that alley right over there? Ray patted Kane on the shoulder, pointing. "I dumped Todd ... what the fuck was his last name? Todd Rogers—that was the sorry nigga's name. I threw his ass in a dumpster down there a few houses down. There used to be an old garage right there, but it was torn down. That nigga tried to fuck me over a few thousand dollars. You believe that stupid shit? I had to make an example of his ass.

"The strange thing was, the police never came or nothing. I had this hoe that I was fuckin' ready wit' an alibi and everything. After Todd, I knew that I was running shit 'cause he had a serious rep as being a hard-ass nigga way back in the day. Shit, that nigga begged for his life from the second I pulled out the bat and starting wailing on his ass wit' it. I beat the nigga like he stole somethin' ... that's right, he did steal something! I beat him until his eye popped out and fell into his lap."

Ray laughed and Kane could feel the chill in his uncle's voice. He loved the stories that Ray would tell about killin' niggaz; it motivated him to be harder. He molded himself to be as hard as his uncle, and then some—a gangsta's gangsta.

The dilapidated housing projects passed by Ray's window, with little kids playing ball and skipping rope in their small, tattered yards and in the street. A small girl chased a puppy between clumps of dead grass and a patchwork of empty, dry dirt and cracked concrete.

Kane continued to watch Ray through the rear-view mirror, considering how best to tell him the information of which he had just gotten wind. "Ray, that was Terry Allen with *The Washington Post* a few minutes ago. He wanted to put a bug in yo' ear about some shit he saw last night."

K. Roland Williams

"What did he see?" Ray continued to stare out the window, unconcerned.

"Well, Terry was covering a story for the Night Life section and was at Victor's penthouse last night. Victor was having a listening party for one of his new acts and it seems yo' boy Quincy was there ... that's not all either, he got out of one of Vic's cars as a guest, walked up through security like a celeb and the whole fuckin' nine. Terry knows him from seeing him at the club and recognized him right away. He thought you might find that interesting. He has pictures of the whole thing. He said he would drop off a few at the club tonight. He told me to tell you it would be his pleasure."

Ray sat silent for a few minutes wrapped in the truck's black leather seats and contemplated what it all meant. He allowed it all to tumble through his head like dirty clothes in a washing machine. "Is that right? That boy can't be that stupid, can he? Yo, pull over here for a second," he requested, almost in a whisper.

Ray rolled down the window and motioned to a few kids playing catch to come over to the truck's window to collect a small stack of twenty-dollar bills he produced from his pocket. The kids excitedly snatched the crisp bills and ran away laughing as the truck slowly pulled away from the curb.

"That would explain why yo' girl was there the other night, probably checking on Quincy and the band, maybe scheming to make him an offer. He must think

K. Roland Williams

you some kind of punk or some shit, Ray." Kane smiled, knowing that he was instigating.

"Well, I definitely can't have nobody fuckin' up my cash flow. Quincy brings in way too much dough to stop now. Besides, I already put down twenty-five grand for studio time downtown. Get that crooked-ass cop on the phone, we need to put his ass to work. I need to get my money's worth from him, too. Motherfuckas just can't let me be a nice guy. They want to play wit' my money, and that just won't work!"

Kane hit a number set into the speed dial of his mobile phone.

"District police," the voice on the other end said.

"Yeah, I need to speak to a Detective Renaldy ... Jack Renaldy in narcotics."

Δ Δ Δ Δ

"Yo, yo, yo, what's up fellas?" Quincy walked into Xavier's apartment five minutes early for this rehearsal, but a day late for the one he missed yesterday and the band was pissed. When Q walked in, Marcel looked at Robert and then at Xavier, who sat behind the Korg keyboard and was the only man in the room smiling.

"Nice for you to show up this time, Q-man. To what do we owe the pleasure?" Xavier was pleased that the guys had finally taken his side and were angry with the fact that he had missed rehearsal without making as much as a call to let anyone know shit. Xavier had been working on them here and there, twisting shit up and throwing salt in Q's game every chance he got. Apparently, it was working 'cause you would have thought Quincy had spat on each one of the guys based on the cold way they were acting.

The room had a fog that Quincy sensed the second he walked in. He could feel the tension in the room. It was like D.C. humidity in the heart of summer.

"A'ight, yaw. Here it is ... I know everybody pissed and shit, and you have good reason to be upset. I broke my own fuckin' cardinal rule, and I want to say I'm sorry for that. It won't happen again." Q looked each man in the eye to show his depth of concern and sincerity.

"Quincy, you haven't missed a rehearsal in years, let alone not call to let us know what was up. That's a no-no." Marcel rubbed his gut, his droopy eyes giving him the appearance of a big black hound dog behind the set of drums.

"Yeah, Q, you should have called or something," Robert said in a disappointed tone. "I could have stayed at home with my wife instead of coming all the way out here to X's crib for no damn reason. You know how much gas costs now—your president got shit all fucked up. It's a long haul from Germantown." He spun his wedding ring around subconsciously as he spoke. "X is right, you have been trippin' lately."

"Is that right? What else has X been telling you

K. Roland Williams

brothas, huh?" He looked at Xavier, who still sat smirking. Q walked slowly toward the trio of men, trying to think of a way to tell them about what happened at the club with Ray and Kane, the threats, the promise of studio time, the gun to his head. Not to mention the newest shit happening with Antoinette Sweet and the potential record deal. It seemed like the right time, but it seemed like the wrong time, too. Maybe if he shared the truth, they would understand. He was vexed.

Before he could open his mouth to tell them the tale, Xavier chimed in. "Well, Quincy, it would seem that the band and I have come to a decision."

"What kind of decision, Xavier?" Quincy could see the bullshit coming, and he began to brace himself for it.

"Well, due to the fact that we were more or less forced to take you on as the leader of this group, I think ... *we* think, that it should go back to the way it used to be, the way it should be again."

"What the fuck are you talking about, X? Spit dat shit out, nigga!" Quincy was losing control. There had been way too much drama going on, and he hadn't had much sleep, or the proper amount of time to process it. He was like a steaming kettle about to blow.

"We had a vote for me to go back to leading this group. I will make the arrangements, sing the leads, write my own lyrics and handle the business for the band."

"You mean handle the money, don't you, X?"

"Well, yeah, I guess so. That's a part of the business, ain't it?" X said sarcastically.

"First of all, how you niggaz gonna have any type of vote without all of us here? What kind of bullshit is that?"

"Well, Q," Marcel said, "You have been distant lately, almost impossible to get in contact with, and pretty damn bossy and shit. We used to do shit as a group, now you write the songs and we just supposed to do what the fuck you say. Frankly, nigga, I think you lettin' all this limelight shit go to your head."

"First of all, you cats know damn well that I had nothing to do wit' the decision in the first place! That was a Raymond James call!"

"Well then, there should be no problem with letting the lead position go," X said with his normal smirk. "Let me deal wit' Ray."

"How do you think you gonna jus' deal wit' Ray? Nobody deals wit' Ray ... but Ray!" Quincy yelled as he paced Xavier's floor like a panther. He clenched his fists, transforming them into hammers, wanting to bash Xavier in his face until he saw the white meat.

"Look, X, dis ain't no fuckin' game! You know that Ray ain't to be fucked wit'! Trust me, you might want to rethink this whole thing." Quincy thought again about telling the guys about the disturbing incident with Kane and Raymond, and then the opportunity with Antoinette Sweet, but since they were acting like little bitches, he figured he would just go forward with his own plans and

K. Roland Williams

allow his boys to take care of themselves. They acted like they had no clue as to what extent Raymond would go to get his way.

"It's like that then, X?" Quincy asked, upset.

"It's like that, Q." Xavier took on a smug look and stood there, arms crossed, waiting to rebut Quincy's next question.

"A'ight, X. Have it your way. Both of you guys feel the same way, huh?"

Marcel and Robert looked at X and back to Quincy. Both men nodded their heads yes and lowered their eyes, now feeling uncomfortable about the decision that X convinced them to make, but not having had the balls to go against it.

"There you go, bruh, it's not like we want you out of the band. You just need to take a step down and let me take things back to the way they used to be."

"The way it used to be, Xavier? You mean before Ray *made* me take over the band and before Neecy came to work at the club. You jealous-ass muthafucker!" Quincy looked Xavier up and down in judgment, wondering why he hadn't seen this bullshit coming a mile away.

Before Quincy lost his mind, he decided to walk out. He could say *fuck them all* and take Antoinette up on her offer. There had been way too much going on lately and the slightest thing, though this lack of loyalty was far from slight, could ruin his friendships for good.

"You know what, yaw niggaz deserve each other.

K. Roland Williams

Understand this though, I am the draw at the fuckin' club ... me! Not you, X. The bitches come to see me perform. So when the droves of people stop coming through the door, be sure to explain that shit to Ray 'cause you about to definitely fuck up his money. Later for you, niggaz!"

"Later for you, Quincy!" X yelled behind Q as he walked out of the apartment and allowed the screen door to slam closed behind him.

Quincy jumped in his rimmed-up Nissan Altima and screeched away from the curb with mixed feelings. The fact that Q never had to explain his problem with Ray at the club, the party at Antoinette's house and the possible record deal made him breathe a sigh of relief. Nevertheless, he also knew that he didn't have a lot of time.

Quincy dialed Antoinette's cell number from his Blackberry.

"Hello," she said in a hushed voice.

"It's me. If you still want to meet, I know a spot."

K. Roland Williams

t e n

Quincy arranged to meet Antoinette at the Starbucks that he frequented in northeast D.C. It was an historic part of town. Its aged brownstones and row houses stood along the street fronts like red brick towers. Wrought-iron gates and carefully painted façades brought back the beauty of this century-old neighborhood. Residents could still walk the streets at night without the fear of crime.

The Starbucks was always full. The tech-savvy crowd gathered there with their iPods and laptops to surf the net and find solitude for school work or meet with friends to discuss various subjects in small groups. He would go there when he wanted to write lyrics to a new song or to reflect a bit on life, a recent break up or his future.

The soothing music piping over the loud speaker system created a sense of calm in Q. He glanced down casually at his black and gold Movado and noticed that

Toni was running ten minutes late, but who was counting? She would add another aspect to this scenario, and Q was anxious to start putting the pieces of this fascinating puzzle together.

Antoinette's silver CL500 Mercedes coupe eventually pulled up past the window to the Starbucks. Quincy saw the car but couldn't see her through the smoked-out tinted windows of the whip. She parked half a block down the street and around the corner adjacent to the Bank of America. He separated the blinds but didn't see her. Q left his seat at the table closest to the front door and walked out along the sidewalk, brushing past the outside patrons of the Starbucks who sat dining under their large patio umbrellas, despite the humidity of the summer afternoon.

Antoinette strolled around the corner in heels, wrapped in an ivory Chanel suit and shades. The hourglass shape of her hips was unmistakable even through the thin, soft fabric of her skirt. She carried a black crocodile briefcase in her hand. The second her eyes fell on Quincy, her soft honey-colored lips parted, greeting him with a bright and inviting smile that contradicted her earlier troubled tone on the phone.

Quincy smiled in return and welcomed her warm hug. Antoinette purred hello. A sweet wisp of perfume floated up to Quincy's nose, and he allowed it to linger there before he exhaled. He thought he felt her hand brush against his ass.

K. Roland Williams

Neither Antoinette nor Quincy noticed the black Lexus 400 sedan that pulled up across the street. Jet black limo tinted windows veiled Ricky Wright as he sat and watched the two through the car window. Spying for Victor was one of Ricky's many jobs. This service happened to be one of the less stressful tasks that he performed for his partner and friend in crime.

Ricky pulled deeply on the Phillies blunt and glanced down at the Desert Eagle that sat loaded next to him on the leather passenger seat. Thick smoke drifted out of the partly-opened moon roof.

Antoinette sipped on a cup of Tazo Green Tea as she pulled the two-inch thick stack of documents from her crocodile briefcase. Her five carat solitaire diamond was flawless to the naked eye and quickly caught the attention of several of the ladies at the table across from them, who, though aware they were being rude, could not keep their eyes off of her ring finger.

"Damn, that's quite some rock you have there," Quincy said.

She spun the platinum band 360 degrees around the circumference of her ring finger.

"Yeah, well, it keeps the dogs away half of the time, the other half—well, they just don't give a shit, and they try and spit game anyway."

Quincy could tell by the conversation she had street smarts; she probably hadn't been born rich. She looked down at the stone and seemed to reminisce briefly on

K. Roland Williams

the good times that the ring used to represent, but no smile accompanied her thoughts, and it seemed that those good times were long gone now.

Sliding the contract over to Quincy, she changed the subject and they started going over some of the details. They discussed recoupable fees, mechanical royalties and points on the album. The conversation went on for over two hours, and though Quincy was knowledgeable about the business side of the music industry, he still knew the importance of running a copy of the contract by someone who wasn't out to totally fuck him like Antoinette Sweet might be. She was the wife of the label owner, and the thought occurred to Quincy that Victor may use her to soften niggaz up. Have them thinking about pussy instead of taking care of business. It came as a surprise to Q when Toni agreed to allow him the time to take the contract to his attorney for a professional opinion.

"Now, I don't want to look a gift horse in the mouth, but I have to ask you why you're giving me this opportunity without any serious preproduction or professional representation?"

"Every now and again, an artist gets a contract on the spot based on their talent alone. You've heard the stories, Quincy. A group sneaks backstage after a concert, corners some really big act, begs to sing live for them, hits the right notes and the next thing you know they're in the studio, filming videos and thanking Jesus at the

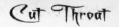

Soul Train Awards. Miracles do happen. Besides, I'm in charge of A&R, and I went out of my way to rush this process for you."

She took another sip of the now-cold tea and pushed the cup away across the small, round table.

"I will have an answer for you no later than the end of this week," Quincy said excitedly.

Now would be a good time for Quincy to tell her about the other contract Raymond had forced him to sign, but he figured that it could wait until he gave it a little more thought. Once the conversation wrapped up and Q's head could not retain any more information, the conversation segued into topics that were more personal.

Δ Δ Δ Δ

Ricky Wright sat impatiently in the black sedan across from the Starbucks. His blood-red eyes focused on Quincy and Antoinette through the window as they talked. The yellowed blinds of the Starbucks window were opened. This afforded Ricky a clear view of the two talking, and everything appeared legit enough.

The light on his Bluetooth earpiece came to life. He pressed the talk button and Victor Sweet's voice crackled loudly through the speaker. Victor questioned his right-hand man on his wife's whereabouts and activities.

Ricky could hear giggling in the background. He

K. Roland Williams

turned the thundering bass down on his Alpine's system so that he would not miss a word.

"Vic, everything looks all right so far. She stopped by the office, stopped by the bank and then came across to the northeast and met that dude from the other night who was at your party."

"What dude, nigga? There was over a hundred niggaz at that party. Am I a psychic or some shit?"

"The pretty boy that she went to see play at *you know who's* club Saturday night, the one she wants to sign."

"Oh all right, I know all about it. He's got the look, but we still have yet to see what he can do."

"Well, just so you know, it looks like she picked up one of the contracts from your safe and handed it to him. I think she has already made up her mind that she is going to sign him with or without your approval."

"First of all ..." Vic hesitated and yelled for the woman that he was with to get the fuck off him until he was done with the phone call.

"First of all, *I* own this label, and I have the final say on who is signed and who is not ... not my fuckin' wife! Can you see her from where you are? Tell me exactly what she does." Victor snapped his cell phone from its cradle on the pants that lay at the foot of another woman's bed and dialed his wife's mobile number. Ricky watched her through the blinds as she lifted her cell phone out of her briefcase, glanced down at the caller ID and pressed a button, apparently disconnecting the call.

K. Roland Williams

"She just hung up on you," Ricky responded with an evil smile, making the matter worse.

"She what?" Vic let her long message play through. He was so pissed he started talking before the message beep had fully stopped.

"I suggest you put down that contract and answer the damn phone. Call me back on my cell." He disconnected the call without as much as a good-bye.

Vic picked the landline back up, warning Ricky to follow them and not to lose them for any reason; he wanted a full report. The phone went silent and Ricky rolled another joint.

Δ Δ Δ Δ

Toni led the discussion like a pro. Taking advantage of Quincy's desire to become a superstar, she allowed him to open up and manipulated the conversation so that by the end, he had her convinced that he was prepared to do *whatever* it took to be successful. She reeled him in like a fish on a hook. Knowing that his desire to be a star would overpower his good judgment, Antoinette batted her eyelashes and threw on the sex appeal. She needed to get closer to make this man obey her, and though she had never cheated on her husband, now would be as good a time as any.

Antoinette excused herself and walked into the ladies' room, taking her cell phone with her. When the

K. Roland Williams

call came through, she knew exactly who it was on the other end. She also knew that Vic always tripped whenever she didn't answer the fuckin' phone on the first ring, but she could usually give a good enough reason for it. He could be over protective, insecure and crazy— a horrible combination. Throw a little cocaine into the mix with a gun, and you had an all-out fool and possibly a dead wife.

After checking her messages, she realized Vic had mentioned that she should put down the contract and call him. *How does he know I have a contract in front of me? He couldn't know that,* she thought. She tapped her foot and twisted the thick curl that hung down over her right eye as she always did when she was perplexed about something.

Rushing back to the table, she urged Quincy to get up and make his way to the door. Only then did she notice the black Lexus that sat motionless across the street with the chrome DUB twenty-threes and the muffled thumping bass, Little John thumping his well-known *yeah, what,* and *okays* loud out of the six-by-nine speakers.

"Ricky," she said to herself. She had to improvise. "He wants to have me followed, then let's give him a reason to be paranoid!"

Quincy was not quite sure what was going on, but he went with it. "It was the call you just got, right?"

He dropped a five on the table, swept the contract up

K. Roland Williams

and headed for the door of the coffee house with Antoinette Sweet close behind.

Ricky hadn't noticed the two get up from the table as he slid another CD into the slot of his stereo, puffing on the freshly rolled fat Purple Haze joint. What he *did* finally notice was the empty window that just a moment before had framed Vic's wife.

"Shit!" He jumped out of the car and trotted to the window he had been staring through for the past two hours. They were nowhere to be seen.

Antoinette and Quincy had just made it around the corner of Seventeenth Street, just east of the Starbucks. Antoinette peeked around the yellow brick retaining wall of the bank and saw Ricky briskly walking into the door. It wouldn't take him long to figure out that they had left already.

"Did you drive?" she asked Quincy.

"Yeah, I parked over there." Q pointed to his black Nissan that sat adjacent to Toni's Benzo.

"Would you mind riding with me right now? I'll bring you to get your ride later. This is a good neighborhood, your car should be cool," she said. "Get in." She fingered the remote control, the car hummed to life, the trunk rose silently and she threw the briefcase inside.

"Come on, come on," she said. That anxious voice was present again as it was earlier on the phone. "Hurry up and get in."

"Hold up a minute, what's going on?" Quincy stood

K. Roland Williams

there in his baggy Sean John jeans and black T-shirt, holding the door open and refusing to get in until she came clean and explained what the fuck was going on.

"I'll tell you everything, just get into the car."

Defiantly, he waited a few more moments, looking at the woman and growing more concerned by the second. He started to think that there *was* some real serious shit going on with her. He wanted to say fuck it all and walk away. Walk away from the contract, his shot at the big time and the woman, but when he looked into her eyes, he couldn't help himself.

Quincy also knew that he couldn't afford any more drama in his life at the moment. Raymond was enough to deal with, with his contracts and power trips. And yet, something about her strength and beauty mixed with this unexplained fear fascinated Quincy to the core. He had to ride with her, and he had to see why a woman who seemed to have it all was so afraid. The music also called to him. Despite all of his *many* priorities, his music still remained at the top of the list, and he had to follow where it led.

The Mercedes pulled off like a bolt, testing the power of the V-12 engine's "zero to sixty miles per hour in less than five seconds" claim.

"Okay, here I am, you have me hostage now ... will you talk to me?"

"Yes, but not yet. Tell me how to get to your place. We can talk there."

K. Roland Williams

They drove as quickly as the convertible Mercedes' chromed AMG wheels could carry them. Antoinette nervously swerved in and out of the afternoon traffic. "Shit," she said, "they're gonna have to get out of my way!"

Quincy found the seat belt to his right and pulled it down. He heard the metallic click and tugged on it to make sure the belt was indeed secure; the woman was driving like the proverbial bat out of hell.

"Okay, get ready to slow down to make this right on Twenty-Fourth," he said, now supporting his weight with his elbow hard against the black leather armrest.

Antoinette slowed just enough to negotiate the sharp turn, and the car's Pirellis squealed in protest of the dangerous speeds.

"Where now?" she asked.

"Go down three more blocks and make a left on L Street. I'm in the second building on the right, but you can pull around to the back off of the street to park." He tried to sound reassuring.

The car lurched to a complete stop in the alley behind Quincy's apartment building. The alley was silent and empty, the only movement was a black and white tabby cat that peeked around a large dumpster, crouched and jumped inside the dirty can.

"Tell me what the fuck is up, Toni!" Quincy gave her his most imposing gaze.

Antoinette looked down into her lap and began to

K. Roland Williams

cry. She laid it on thick, the tears rolling down her cheek and along the gentle curve of her chin, finally dropping to her suit's lapel.

Quincy felt sad for the woman. Though he had only known her for a few days, he knew from day one at the party that something was going on in her life that was very complicated and very difficult for her to deal with. He placed his hand on her right shoulder then slid it to the back of her silky neck. She felt warm, the adrenaline from the drive obviously still pulsing through her veins.

"Whatever the problem is, it will be all right. I'll be here for you if you need me to," Quincy said.

She turned to Quincy and placed her hand on his left leg. "Okay, here's the deal. When we were in the Starbucks and my phone rang, it was my husband. He said something that led me to believe that his friend was following me. He was actually outside of the Starbucks while we were there."

"Did you see him or his car? Were we just being followed?" Quincy looked in the rear-view and side mirrors of the Mercedes.

"I'm not sure. The car in front of the Starbucks could have been Ricky's, but shit, they change cars like most folks change underwear. The song that I heard coming from the car was muffled, but it was a Cut Throat recording. I'm pretty damn sure of it, and if I'm right, it hasn't been released yet, so he is one of the few people who could be playing it right now."

K. Roland Williams

"Well, I still don't understand ... we weren't doing anything wrong, we were just going over the contract. If that's the case we could have done that at the office."

"Well, that's not the point. Vic doesn't know you yet, so he doesn't trust you. Besides that, I told him I went to get my nails done."

"Why'd you lie about that?"

"You don't know him. He's crazy. I can't go to the bathroom without him having to know when I'm coming back and what I did when I was in there. So I just thought that it would be easier to tell him something safer. Now I look like I'm up to something."

"Well, this won't be good for me. He probably won't go through with the deal now."

Antoinette looked around the alley again, making sure that they were still alone. "Can we please go up to your apartment for a while? I need time to think this through."

Antoinette's cell phone went off at that exact moment. She didn't even look at it, just fingered the power button and dropped it into the Benz's leather armrest. "I'll talk to him when I talk to his ass. He's probably with another bitch right now anyway."

"Hey, we'll get though his shit. I'm sure it's just some crazy misunderstanding, come on." He got out, went around to her side, and opened the driver's side door.

Quincy's building was an old nineteenth century number with New York City brownstone qualities. His apartment was located on the third floor in the back of the building, facing the rear alley. They walked past neatly painted doors with brass kick plates, numbers and knockers, each one neatly and uniformly placed.

Quincy unlocked the three dead bolts that secured his front door, the last one not wanting to open without a fight. "You've got to jiggle this one," Quincy said, wrestling and twisting the key around in the keyhole, slightly embarrassed. The lock eventually gave up its battle with a *click, clack,* and Quincy opened the door on squeaky hinges. With a flip of the switch, the foyer light was on, revealing a very clean, well-furnished apartment. He locked the door behind them.

"You have a very nice bachelor pad here," Toni said, "and I love the leather sectional. Very neat, very sexy."

"Thanks, but I'm sure your shoe closet is bigger than this."

"No, it's about half this size." They paused for a second and broke out into loud laughter. Once they stopped laughing, the giggles trailed off into uncomfortable silence. Antoinette took off her suit jacket and handed it to Quincy to hang up.

"Can I get you anything?" Quincy asked.

"No, I'm good," she said, finally removing her expensive shades, hoping her eyes weren't still puffy from crying earlier in her car.

"Well, I'm glad to see that you feel better. You were starting to worry me."

K. Roland Williams

"Yeah, I'm all better now," she said with a grin. She dropped her purse on the coffee table in the living room.

"You know what, Q? On second thought I *would* like something."

"Anything, just tell me," he said.

"Do you have any wine in there?" She pointed a perfectly French manicured finger toward the kitchen.

"Sure, I do. Now what kind of host would I be without a decent bottle of Merlot or Zinfandel for a guest?" Quincy gave Antoinette a warm smile as he entered the kitchen. "Make yourself at home." He pointed to the contemporary black sectional in the center of the living room. "The bathroom is down the hall and to the right if you need to use it."

"Oh, I intend on making myself a *lot* more comfy," she said under her breath.

Quincy proceeded to pull out a bottle of Merlot, rinse out the last two matching wine glasses he had to his name and pop the cork on the bottle. Moving into the living room with the glasses, he sat on the couch and found the remote control to his stereo. He could hear the water softly trickling in the bathroom and was glad to see that his guest was indeed making herself comfortable.

After a sip or two of the wine he turned on the stereo, found a nice jazz track, and began to hum to the melody. The tenor sax and mean bass line serenaded him and prompted him to start formulating a song in his head.

K. Roland Williams

"Are you okay in there?" he said loudly over the music. Toni did not respond.

Antoinette silently and cautiously made her way to the back of the couch behind Quincy as he sat with his eyes held closed and bobbed his head to the soothing jazz. She ran her fingers through his soft, curly hair and passionately kissed the crown of his head.

"Oh, what's up, girl? I was about to start worrying about you." Quincy turned around to face Antoinette and found her standing there with nothing on but a black garter, stockings and her three-inch stilettos.

"Damn, baby," he said, wide-eyed, as he came to his feet, taking in the woman's curves. Her tight shape could have gone up against any model or video chick Quincy had ever laid eyes on.

"Well, Quincy, you told me to get more comfortable, so here I am." Her voice rolled like soft brown velvet and her eyes were trained on Quincy's expression with naughty curiosity. "Are you going to just stand there and stare at me, or are you going to do something?"

Quincy crossed the sectional with one large step and joined Antoinette on the far side. He grabbed her firmly and cupped her face in his hands, burying his mouth into hers, feasting on her lips and tongue. She moaned and fed him what he desired. Sucking in his full lips, she sank into his strong muscular arms. Toni had known some-how from the second she saw him singing on the stage, probably by the way the man moved, that he would

K. Roland Williams

excite her and make her body tremble with his every touch.

Quincy picked her straight up into his arms and carried her to his bedroom. Laying Toni down on the bed, he kissed her from the top of her head to the soles of her perfectly pedicured feet. He stared intimately into her light brown eyes and grabbed a handful of her long, silky hair and tugged her head back firmly, allowing his tongue to dance slowly across her warm neck. Then he moved down to her nipples, which ached and throbbed for Quincy's mouth.

Quincy took his time with her. Kissing every inch of her trembling flesh, he lifted Toni's long brown leg in the air and admired the firm muscles of her thigh and calf. The pumps she still wore were sexy as hell, and Quincy could feel his dick beginning to throb rigid and heavy in his silk boxers. Before he could reach down and remove his pants, she had already begun to go to work on the buttons of his jeans, unsnapping them and skillfully pulling his pants down to expose his fully erect manhood.

Her eyes grew large with the sight of his swollen cock, and she smiled the mischievous grin of a child unwrapping an early Christmas gift.

"Damn, baby, it's like that?" she purred.

They went on kissing, sucking and licking for what seemed like hours.

Eventually, she allowed him to enter her warm, wet,

K. Roland Williams

starving pussy, and he did so slowly and skillfully.

She moaned, arched her back and threw her pelvis forward, allowing Quincy to penetrate her fully. He buried himself inside of her until she thought she could not take another inch of his stiffness. It ached with a sweetness that Antoinette had never known, even with her very own husband. She threw herself to him in perfect sync and matched his every smooth movement.

Insatiable passion overtook the pair as they went at each other under the whirling ceiling fan with jazz playing distantly in the background. At that moment, they were oblivious to time and space, and totally, utterly engulfed inside of each other, as one. They groped each other animalistically and drowned inside of their deepest desires, probing and exploring every inch of their starving bodies. Riding the crest of ecstasy, they reached climax together and held on tight as they free fell through space, their senses sharp, their hearts like one large beating drum.

Their bodies stiffened together, exploded, then fell apart, dripping with the sweat and sweet sensation of deep fulfillment. They finally began to breathe again, after what seemed like an eternity. Kissing slowly and passionately like life-long lovers, they held one another and fell into the deepest, most gratifying sleep of their lives.

K. Roland Williams

eleven

What ... you lost her? How in the fuck ... what do I pay you for?" Victor's anger was nothing new to Ricky. He had heard him that mad before over a variety of topics and this was no different. He removed his diamond-laced Versace frames and set them on the dashboard of his Lex, acting as if he were listening to the scolding that his boss was giving him.

"Yeah, she got away. What do you want me to do now?"

"What da fuck you mean, *what do you want me to do now*? I want yo' ass to find my fuckin' wife!" Victor yelled into the phone.

Victor slammed the cell closed and turned to the naked woman who sat at his feet waiting to serve him. Once Victor put the phone down on the side table, Desiree attempted to go back to work pleasing him in any way he desired. Victor snatched away from her in anger. He thought back to a time when Antoinette was still hustling high rollin' niggaz out of their dough. She had never been stupid and always found a way to get want she wanted. *Shit*, Victor thought, *she found a way to get at my ass.* Whatever she wanted with Quincy had Victor concerned, more concerned than he had been in a long time.

Δ Δ Δ Δ

Insecure-ass nigga, Ricky thought. *Victor knows how he stole Antoinette in the first damn place, that's why he can't trust her to go to the corner store without me following her ass.*

Ricky struck a match, put it to the end of his Phillies blunt and took in a deep pull of the thick gray smoke. He held it for several seconds before releasing the strong aroma into the cab of his car. He turned his Alpine stereo's bass up until it thumped the side mirrors so much that it distorted his view. "Yeah, just right," he smiled, bobbing his neck to the music.

Δ Δ Δ Δ

Quincy knew he had to come clean with Antoinette about the contract and his legal obligation to Raymond James, and now seemed to be as good a time as any to do it. Q was no dummy when it came to women, and he knew that a mere fuck didn't mean any type of serious

K. Roland Williams

commitment or relationship, but he still felt obligated to share the information with her. She obviously knew more about Raymond then she was willing to share—the first night he saw her at the club proved that—and this might be the right time to discuss the details.

"Look, I appreciate the opportunity that you are giving me, I really do. But check it, I haven't told you the whole story about the deal I made with Raymond, the owner of the club where I play." Antoinette nuzzled into Quincy's chest and slid her hand down the shaft of his penis, trying to caress it back to life for the third time in a row, acting as if she didn't hear him. "Did you hear me? I have something serious that I want to talk to you about, and it might throw a wrench in my chance to sign with your label."

She removed her hand from underneath the covers and sighed, disappointed she had to wait for the third session of screwing. "You have my every attention," she said with a sly grin. "Go for it."

"I signed a contract with Raymond to play at his club for another five years ... exclusively."

"Well, that *could* be a problem," she smirked. "Ray can be a real asshole when it comes to legal shit."

"Wait a minute, you know Raymond?" Q tried to act surprised about the fact that she knew him.

"Well, put it this way, I have had dealings with him in the past, but nothing that you should concern yourself with. Remember, I'm in the music business, he's in the

109

club business, and they go hand in hand."

Sensing that there was more to the story, Quincy demanded more information about their past dealings together, but Toni remained elusive with her explanation.

"Raymond is, or can be, a dangerous man, and I'm sure he won't appreciate me just up and leaving the deal like this. It's a violation of the contract that I signed with him, not to mention he could take this to court if he wanted to, and if I'm lucky that's all he'll want to do. Are you sure Victor will want to deal with this sort of problem? He could just as easily move on and find someone else for this project of yours."

"Listen, Quincy, artists break contracts in our business more often than you might think, and there are ways around that—legally, of course. If it was another label you had signed with, then it would be a totally different dilemma, but Raymond ... please." She rolled her eyes and sucked her teeth hard, which validated even further that she knew him better than she was willing to admit. "I could throw him twenty-five grand and the whole thing would probably go away. That nigga all about the Benjamins, don't get it twisted. He will just find someone else to replace you and your band anyway. Don't worry, Sweetie, I got you." She winked her eye and smiled a dazzling smile.

Quincy absorbed her advice and found that it did, in some small way, ease his mind. "Yeah, I guess there is

K. Roland Williams

nothing that a little cash can't handle in today's world, huh?" he said.

"That's right, baby, don't sweat it. Let momma handle that." She allowed her fingertips to gently trace a path across his face. "Don't worry about it."

But Quincy did have something to worry about. Besides Raymond and dealing with this broken contract shit, he had just slept with the wife of the owner of the label who seemed to be serious about offering him a record deal. And to add fuel to the already hot fire, Victor Sweet was equally as dangerous as Ray, maybe more so. Quincy needed to slow down and think it out, though using Antoinette to get a little closer to what he want-ed—shit, *needed*—was a risk that was worth taking. Fuck it. He turned to Antoinette, and she slid her tongue out slowly between her lips, teasing him. Quincy took her hand and placed it on his hard dick that pushed up from underneath the Egyptian cotton sheets like a periscope.

"I see you're ready for round three," she said with a wicked smile on her face. She stroked his shaft harder and faster now, forcing more blood into his already engorged member until it throbbed hard and hot in her hand.

Quincy moaned in delight as she pulled back the sheets and put her tongue to work up and down his dick. She took him totally and hungrily into her hot mouth, slowly and deliberately stroking him with her hand until he thought he might explode. Her deep throat game was

K. Roland Williams

the shit, and Quincy's eyes rolled back in his head as he enjoyed her skills.

Quincy knew that Toni was gaming him to some degree, but he was willing to get into the mix and play this thing out to the end. He had a lot riding on it now and really couldn't turn back. Nevertheless, he would have to really keep an eye on this woman. Quincy lay there moving his hips in sync with her hands and mouth, closed his eyes and smiled.

K. Roland Williams

twelve

Quincy and Antoinette casually walked out of his apartment and into the hot, humid night air. It was getting late, and Toni knew that Vic would be livid when she got home, but she didn't really give a fuck at the moment. Her major concern was that she had accomplished step one of her plan to get Quincy out of Ray's grasp. If she could bring him on board with Cut Throat she would get Ray's attention in the worst way, and knowing him, he would react quickly and take it directly to Victor. Victor wouldn't have a chance without the back up of a bad-ass crew like the one Ray employed. There was no way Victor and Ricky could take on those hard-ass niggaz who still ran with Raymond and Kane.

The two walked toward her Mercedes to find a black Crown Victoria sitting behind her vehicle, blocking her into the space.

"Hey, it looks like the guy is in there. I'll ask him to move out of your way." Quincy walked up and tapped on the tinted glass. The window came down to expose the face of a heavyset, middle-aged white man who looked up and smiled at Quincy.

"Hey, can you move your car so we can get out?" Quincy asked.

"Sure can, in a minute." The white man looked at Quincy, opened the car door without a word and pushed him back with the door.

"Yo, what the fuck's up, man? I asked you to move your car, now you gonna hit me with your door?"

"Are you Quincy Underwood?" the man said calmly.

"It depends on who wants to know." Quincy looked into the car and noticed the laptop propped up and the multiple antennas on the unmarked vehicle, making it clear that it was a police car.

"Oh, excuse me for being rude. My name is Jack Renaldy. I am a detective with narcotics ... Metro P.D."

"Whoa, what's this about? I just say no to drugs, bruh." Quincy took a step backward.

Renaldy drew his weapon and told Quincy to stay still and not to move.

Toni was horrified, thinking that Victor had sent the cop. She began to back away.

"Aren't you a married woman ... Mrs. Sweet, I presume? Victor Sweet's wife? What do you think he would say if he knew you were leaving this young man's house?"

"What's this shit about, cop? I told you I don't fuck

K. Roland Williams

wit' no drugs," Quincy said in his defense.

"I know you don't, but you're going to have to come with me nonetheless." Renaldy, still holding the gun on Quincy, told Antoinette to go home to her husband and assured her that Quincy would be okay. He only needed to answer a few simple questions at the station and then he would be free to go.

"How do you know who I am if my husband didn't send you?"

"Your plates, I ran your plates. I *am* a cop, remember." Renaldy smiled and slid the gun back into the holster. He then pushed Quincy into the back seat of his unmarked cruiser.

"Don't worry, Quincy, I'll get you out if you need me. My cell will be on." Antoinette moved out of the way as the cop backed the car out from behind hers and disappeared around the corner of the alley and out of sight.

"This could be a problem for me," she said as the car pulled away with Q in the back seat.

Δ Δ Δ Δ

Quincy was already confused by the fact that a cop had picked him up and might be charging him with some trumped up bullshit. He knew he hadn't done anything wrong, except fuck another man's wife, but if Victor didn't send the cop, then what was going on? A few minutes later they were passing the precinct building where the

K. Roland Williams

cop said he worked.

"Where are you taking me? You said you worked at the ninth precinct, and we just passed it." Quincy started to get a bit nervous. The streets were now dark and the streetlights seemed to pop on one at a time as the cruiser went under each tall pole.

A mile later, they were turning off the main street and into the parking lot of The Melody Room.

"What the fuck is up with this ... Oh, I see, Raymond sent you to my place to find me."

"Yeah, and you made my life very easy," the cop said. "You were home. I thought I was going to have to sit there staking your apartment building out until early in the morning."

"I don't know what Ray told you but ..."

"Look kid, I don't want to know shit about what's going on. I just suggest whatever Raymond wants with you, do it, and make life easy on yourself." The cop gave Quincy a sincere look through the rear-view mirror. Quincy recognized that look as bullshit. A white cop in a black hood working for Raymond had to amount to bullshit—couldn't be nothing sincere about it.

"Fuck you, you crooked-ass cop." Survival mode began to kick in with Quincy. He knew that whatever this was about, it had to be bad, not to mention the fact that he had just been caught coming out of his place with the wife of Victor Sweet, one of the most notorious niggaz in D.C.

K. Roland Williams

Getting out of the car, Renaldy lit a cigarette. "All right, Mr. Underwood, this is where I leave you in the Lord's hands. Good luck." The cop pointed to the front door of the club, quietly threatening Quincy with his eyes. "And if you run, I *will* put a bullet in your black ass ... we understand each other, boy?" The cop smiled, patting his gun and holster, and shot Quincy a condescending grin. He stayed behind, watching Q walk toward the club.

Q wondered what it would feel like to knock all his teeth down his throat.

"Seems like he's your boss, too ... boy," Quincy said without looking back.

As Quincy entered the large door to the club, he saw the DJ setting up for the night and the waitresses and bartenders stocking the bar. Raymond was nowhere to be found. Quincy stopped for a moment to look for Neecy. He noticed her in the back, cleaning the V.I.P. section of the club, her head low. The other club employees smiled at Q and waved to say what's up as they all continued getting the club ready to open for the night.

"So I guess you think you a celebrity or some shit, huh, pretty boy?" Kane said as he walked up behind Quincy.

"What the fuck are you talking about, Kane?"

"What, you think us ghetto niggaz don't know what the fuck is going on in our own town, like we don't read the newspaper and shit ... look at this." Kane pulled out a few pictures from his pocket and threw them at Quincy. They were pictures of Quincy getting out of the limo and entering Vic and Antoinette Sweet's building for the record release party.

"What, I can't go to a party unless it's here at this club?"

"Don't get smart wit' me. The only reason you're breathing now is because Ray said you can. You're an investment, don't get it twisted. I've killed niggaz for a lot less than the tussle we had upstairs the other night, so consider yourself lucky."

"Good thing I don't believe in luck," Quincy said sarcastically.

Kane started to talk again, but Quincy cut him off mid-sentence, walking up close to the man's scarred face. "Look, nigga, I don't have time for this bullshit. Either you gonna make a fuckin' move or you're not. If you're not, get the fuck out of my way!"

Kane stood there smiling sinisterly, looking at Quincy with the curiosity of a child.

"Look, I don't know why Ray had me fuckin' kidnapped by a cop and brought here, but I got other shit to do. I'm out!"

"You ain't going nowhere, bruh. Ray wants to talk to you, and he should be here in a few minutes." Kane cracked his knuckles and waited for Q's response.

Quincy walked past the man and headed toward the front door. Neecy listened attentively, still acting as if she were cleaning.

Quincy was a few feet from the door when he heard Kane's voice and footsteps following closely behind him.

"Fuckin' snake in a pin-striped suit," Quincy mumbled to himself.

"What the fuck you say, nigga?" Kane shoved Quincy hard toward the front door.

Quincy turned around and without hesitation punched Kane squarely in his jaw, catching him off-guard. Kane absorbed the punch, shook it off and clenched his teeth. He stared at Quincy with his nostrils flared, and then he rushed him. Both men met like cars in a head-on collision. They swung at each other with blows to the face and body. Kane's fist dug deep into Quincy's ribs as he talked shit.

"See, nigga," Kane said as he pounded Q's body with his fist. "This is what you wanted, so now you got it!" Quincy blocked some of the blows and returned his own punches, but Kane was the more experienced fighter. He was able to dip and slide, avoiding most of Q's punches. He was clearly issuing more abuse than he was taking.

As the two men struggled, Kane was able to get his Glock out of its holster. Quincy grabbed his right wrist and held Kane's gun arm up in the air. They wrestled with the weapon. Kane hadn't planned to shoot Q, Ray wasn't having that; his intention was just to get the nigga under control until Ray got there, but now shit was heated and totally out of control. If he had to shoot Quincy,

K. Roland Williams

so be it. The nigga officially had it coming for swinging first.

Neecy watched from a distance. She saw Kane pull his gun and decided she couldn't just stand by and watch Quincy get shot to death right there in front of her. She had to help the man that she was growing to care for. She ran in between them, trying to separate the two. As Kane and Q continued wrestling for the gun, Neecy was thrown down. A small black electronic device fell from underneath her shirt and slid across the dance floor right at Kane's feet.

Pushing Quincy off him he said, "What the fuck, is that ... a wire?" Kane turned his attention and his gun on Neecy. Quincy stood there, hands partially up now that the gun was free and away from his grasp. A thin, crimson stream of blood ran down Kane's chin as he picked up the small black box. A slender wire dangled from it like a severed artery.

"It *is* a wire, some type of recorder ... yo, you a fuckin' cop? What the fuck is going on here?" Kane said to Neecy.

Quincy went to help Neecy up from the floor. She stood quickly, reaching for her ankle holster and pulled a small black semi-automatic while Kane was still focused on the device he held in his hand.

"I'm a special agent with the FBI and you are under arrest!" Neecy aimed her weapon confidently at Kane. Her deep cover was blown, and she had no communica-

K. Roland Williams

tion with the outside world. She had no other choice but to make her move; her life depended on it now.

"Drop the weapon," she said to Kane.

"Look, we can work something out, I'm sure." Kane inched his gun up slowly toward her, hoping to distract her as he talked. Quincy stood next to Neecy, trying to figure out what was going on.

"Quincy, get that phone on the bar and call 911. Tell the operator to connect you to Special Agent Majors at the downtown FBI branch. Have them send the D.C. Metro cops, too."

When Quincy moved toward the bar, Kane told him to stay still. "Don't move a fuckin' muscle. We need to figure this thing out."

"Drop that gun or I *will* put a bullet in your head. Slide it over here," Neecy said to Kane.

"You ain't killin' shit, bitch. You bluffin'!"

"Bluffing ... nigga, I promise you I'm not." Q noticed that Neecy's Southern accent had dissolved along with her cover. She had definitely not been who she said she was, and it was all out in the open now.

Kane acted as if he would comply and lowered his weapon. Before he dropped it to the floor though, he raised the Glock quickly and fired. Neecy discharged her gun at the same time, striking Kane in the shoulder and spinning him around like a rag doll. The small recorder in his hand went flying again, this time sliding under a table next to the dance floor.

K. Roland Williams

Quincy ducked at the sound of the gunfire, and the club employees all ran for cover. Once the smoke cleared, Quincy went to Neecy, who lay in a crumpled heap on the floor in a puddle of thick, dark blood. He lifted her head up off the floor. He was surprised to see a slight smile on her face and a single tear rolling down her cheek.

"Quincy, get the wire." Neecy's voice was labored, her breaths shallow and quick. "There is serious evidence on that tape, hopefully enough to put them all in jail for life."

"Don't talk, baby girl, you're gonna be all right, just don't talk, okay?" Quincy screamed for someone to call an ambulance.

"Quincy, there is more evidence at my apartment ... the agency will know where to go ... make sure the right people get it so we can put Raymond and Kane's asses in jail for life." Her voice was fading into a strained whisper.

"Don't let me go," she said as Quincy gently held her, the aroma of gun smoke still heavy in the air.

"I got you, baby girl, I got you," he told her as his eyes teared up and he continued to softly rock her like a baby. Quincy looked to where Kane had fallen with hatred in his eyes. Kane didn't move. He lay still as a corpse on the club's dance floor, not more than a few feet away from the wire.

Neecy looked up at Quincy and told him, "My name is Diana Lawson, not Neecy. I'm sorry I had to lie to you, Q."

K. Roland Williams

The club employees looked out in terror as Q yelled again for someone to call 911. Q grabbed Neecy's gun from the floor next to her. He focused one eye on the dying agent and one on Kane as he rubbed her head tenderly. Just then, Raymond's voice could be heard as he came loudly down the hallway from the rear entrance.

Neecy's blood engulfed Quincy's leg and arm. He could feel her life leaking out of her in a warm, wet, sticky surge, her beautiful, mink-colored face getting paler by the second.

"Everything wasn't a lie ... I really did want to get to know you better ... not for the job ... I really was feelin' you."

She convulsed and stiffened as Quincy watched her usually bright eyes glaze over and fade out into a lifeless gaze up into the ceiling beyond him. She took her last, labored breath in Quincy's arms, and she died.

Raymond James came around the corner and was shocked. There was his nephew on one side of the dance floor shot up, his bartender—whose name he didn't even know—on the other, bleeding everywhere, and Quincy in the middle of all of it. "What the fuck is going on in my goddamn club?" he growled.

"What's going on in your club is yo' ass is about to go to jail, that's what!" Q laid Neecy's head gently on the floor and jumped to his feet, looking down at her body, unable to comprehend the reality of what had just happened. It was surreal, like an image moving past him in

K. Roland Williams

the distance. He held her Walther P99 to his side loosely in his hand, almost wanting to drop it to the floor. Instinctively, he wanted to run the fuck out of there. But the look in Ray's eyes and seeing Kane there possibly dead on the floor made him think better of it. He knew that Ray would want someone's head for this fiasco, and at that moment, it seemed to Quincy that it might be his. He clenched the gun tighter now. He raised the gun and aimed it at Ray's wide chest. He walked over and picked up the wire, looking at it curiously and holding the gun on Raymond.

"Put that fucking gun down. Get it off of my uncle," Kane said weakly while he stood on buckling legs. "That bitch was a Fed or a cop or some shit, Ray. Look in Quincy's hand, she had a wire." Raymond saw the black box and he couldn't believe his eyes. He had let a cop into his establishment and never had a clue. Thinking quickly, he tried to manipulate the situation the best he could.

"Okay, Q, we can bounce back from this shit. Just keep your cool, man. Don't do anything stupid. I can hand you one hundred thousand for that wire right here and right now. One trip to the safe and you'll be a rich man."

Quincy was trembling and numb, the reality of Neecy's—Diana's—death not sunken in yet. The sound of Ray's voice snapped him out of the trance.

At that moment, Renaldy sheepishly peeked his

K. Roland Williams

flushed red face into the club's front door. He had heard the gunshots and didn't want to rush in blindly without first knowing what he was about to get himself into. As he quickly surveyed the scene, Q saw the light leak into the club from the parking lot lamps. He saw Renaldy looking through the slit in the door, and before the cop could close it, Quincy was on him.

"Yo, cop, don't even think about it. Get in here right now. Don't make me tell you twice." Quincy was close enough to the door, with Neecy's gun pointed his way, to make Renaldy think twice about running. "And don't even think about runnin'. I *will* put a bullet in yo' white ass," Quincy said, wondering if the cop recognized his own brash words from earlier.

"Quincy, let's talk about this. We can fix this shit." Raymond was still trying to reason with Q.

"Yeah, like we talked about the contract that you strong-armed me into signing, Ray? Oh, we gonna fix this shit all right."

Raymond twisted his lips and knew he could not reply.

"Give me the keys to your police car," Q said, knowing it was his only way out of there. Renaldy still stood as if he could pivot on his foot and run out of the club.

"You betta not give him the keys, cop," Kane interjected.

"Give me the keys right now." Q pointed the gun at the cop with seriousness pressing hard against his face.

K. Roland Williams

The cop hesitated briefly and Quincy fired the gun. The bullet zipped past Renaldy's head so closely that he could feel the force from the projectile.

"Goddamn!" Renaldy yelled, ducking. He threw the keys to Q.

With the gun pointed toward the three men and the wire tightly gripped in his hand, he took one last sad look at Neecy's lifeless body and ran out the front door of The Melody Room.

Δ Δ Δ Δ

Antoinette strolled into the bedroom of her luxury penthouse. It was getting late and she dreaded the inevitable conversation with her husband. There was no way of knowing what was going on with Quincy. She hoped he would call her to inform her where he was.

She made her way to the bathroom and turned the brass knob of the shower to its hottest setting, allowing her clothes to trail her into her bedroom one piece at a time, leaving her bra, silk blouse, and panties in a messy line of expensive fabric across the floor. She made her way back to the shower and pulled the frosted glass door back. The steam poured out into the bathroom with a hot hiss. She stepped in, and the water cascaded down over her body as she washed away the sweat that she and Quincy had generated in their passionate sex session just hours earlier.

K. Roland Williams

She could still feel the ache between her legs where he penetrated her pussy over and over again. With this thought, she rubbed the soapy sponge across her still-swollen clit, enjoying the sweet, dull throbbing. As the water swirled around the shower drain, she permitted the thoughts of her own husband to drip away into the far recesses of her mind. She would not be denied her objective; she had gotten far too close. The only obstacle would be Victor. He would be pissed when he saw her, but right now, she didn't really care. She reveled in the happiness of the moment.

The plan, as she envisioned it, was a simple one: she would pit the two killers—Raymond and her husband, Victor—against each other, and Quincy would be the spark that ignited the fire between the two men. She would have to lay it on thick but keep her own sweet ass out of the crossfire, and pray that Raymond would have the upper hand. She realized it was a flawed plan, but it was all she had at the moment and would have to do. She prayed that Raymond's hate for Victor and herself would be enough to throw him over the edge and move on Victor.

With Vic dead and out of the picture, she would be able to control the record label and run things as she saw fit. She would have access to the money, the status and everything else that came with owning a hundred-million-dollar business. The steam from the shower enveloped her body, and she allowed the drama and bitter feelings for her husband to mix in with the warm vapor and dissipate into the air.

Victor followed the trail of clothes that lay spread erratically across their cavernous bedroom. At the end of the pink and black clothing trail, he picked up his wife's silk and rhinestone thong, immediately feeling the dampness in the crotch of the thin fabric. He put it close to his nostrils and inhaled the aroma deeply, rolling the smell through his mental Rolodex of odors. He concluded that this was a mixture of more than one. It wasn't her normally sweet scent, but one more pungent. It smelled like sex.

The waterfall shower in the marble master bath was loud, and he could hear her in there humming, something Vic hadn't heard her do in years. That in itself was very suspicious, downright suspect. Eight hours had gone by since Ricky lost her in front of the Starbucks across town. Victor's anger had long since subsided, but he could feel that familiar pang welling up in his gut again with the thought of her disappearing with that pretty nigga from his party the other night.

The anger that he had gotten so good at controlling since he was a legitimate executive and celebrity was hard to curb. He could feel his old ways welling up again, but the killer in him could not be released with his life constantly under scrutiny by the media, his fans, everybody. Something was going on, and he was determined to find out what it was.

K. Roland Williams

thirteen

Desperate, Quincy grabbed his cell phone and dialed Xavier's number. The answering machine picked up on the fourth ring. Xavier's voice was monotone and requested that the person calling leave a name, number and brief message. Taboo's music was playing in the background. The strange thing was, it wasn't Quincy on lead vocal, but Xavier. *That nigga didn't waste any time taking my voice off lead and replacing it with his own. He must have done it with his little eight channel recorder,* Q thought.

Putting his frustration aside, Quincy scratched his head and waited for the beep.

"Yo, X, it's me. Before you delete this message, I got some serious shit to holla at you about. You need to get at me. There was a problem tonight, Neecy was shot … Listen I can't talk now, so call me the second you get the message."

Quincy hung the phone up and reached into his

pocket to ensure the small black digital recorder was still intact. It was. He pressed the small green button on the top of the device, and a very irritated Raymond James could be heard talking to both Renaldy and Kane:

"Kane, I want you to take this motherfucker out, and make it clean this time. None of that sloppy shit like with that punk-ass nigga, Ronny. I don't want any traces of him found at all. You understand?"

Raymond seemed to be standing right on top of the microphone—his voice was crystal clear. There was no way Neecy could have been so close to this incriminating conversation.

"Tape," Quincy said aloud. She must have taped the recorder to the bottom of Raymond's desk. He fingered the FF button and stopped randomly:

"Now get the fuck out of my office before I really lose my mothafuckin' patience. Kick rocks, nigga, and leave the signature page. Don't forget to read over the contract. I don't want you to feel like I cheated you or no shit."

A chill ran up Quincy's back as he listened to the tape of himself, Ray and Kane that night a few days ago in Ray's office. This was definitely proof that Ray forced Quincy to sign the contract.

Raymond was ranting on about killing another two men several years ago, laughing with Kane about how the two brothas begged for their lives and how Ray and two other guys beat them to death in an alley with baseball bats and a nine iron golf club. They apparently

K. Roland Williams

buried the bodies somewhere way south of Annapolis, in the woods west of the Chesapeake Bay.

"Fuck Ortega. Look, we have been quiet enough over the last year. It's time we shut this town down again!" Raymond yelled at Kane at the top of his voice. His words were loud and clear despite his ruined voice box. *"It's time we find a new supplier anyway. Ortega is a dinosaur and we need somebody closer to home, someone reachable. I would take the motherfucka out myself if I could!"*

Quincy continued to drive and listen to the recording that Neecy made. The more he listened, the more he knew he was in serious trouble. The evidence on the tape would put Ray, Kane and Renaldy in jail for a long time, and though they may not know what Neecy had taped exactly, they damn sure were not gonna stop chasing Q until they found out. They would definitely kill him if they caught him now. The game had moved to the next level, and Quincy had to stay ahead of the game if he wanted to live through the night.

fourteen

"Okay, Renaldy, we need to get this under control. I don't want any fuckin' fallout because this bitch was an undercover!" Raymond pointed at Neecy's body, pale and almost bled out on the dance floor. "We need to get rid of this body and we have to find Quincy's ass ASAP! Quincy is now a fuckin' liability. I want him back here alive if possible, but dead if necessary! He's still an investment of mine, but the wire is the priority—I can find another singer for the band if I have to."

"How do you expect there *not* to be any fallout if she was an agent? They know she's here, and she can't just disappear! For all we know, they have the club under surveillance." Renaldy had his arms up, nervously waving them around in the air.

Kane was getting woozy from blood loss and was battling shock. Raymond steadied his nephew and sat him down at one of the club's tables and looked at Kane's wound. The bullet went in clean and exited the

K. Roland Williams

back of his shoulder just as neatly. A narrow stream of blood still leaked from the hole, snaking down his arm and dripping to the floor.

Kane blacked out for a second and came to, confused. "Shit, what happened?"

"You just killed a cop, genius," Renaldy said sarcastically.

"I got an idea." Raymond called the few employees over that were working that night. The small crowd had stood by the bar and not moved per Ray's instructions. They knew they could end up like Neecy. "Yo, all yaw niggaz get over here right now!"

Kane came to his feet on weak knees. He picked up his gun and slid it into his holster with a wince. "Yeah, get the fuck over here. Reggie, Casey, Kev, Deirdre and Andre, front and fuckin' center!" Kane yelled.

The small, rag-tag group of club employees shuffled over to the blood-covered dance floor, everyone with his or her head down, acting as if nothing had happened and they had not seen a thing.

"A'ight yaw, we don't have long." Ray looked each employee in the eye as he walked down the line like a general inspecting his team of troops.

"Ray, we gotta clean this shit up! This motherfuckin' cop should have known what was going on." Kane groaned in pain, his hand pressed hard against the hole in his shoulder. "Ray, I'm gonna need to get to a doctor real soon."

K. Roland Williams

"Man-up, Kane," Ray growled, "we have some bigger shit going on here. I'll send you to one of my on-call doctors in a second. But right now, we have to clean up this mess. Well, what do you have to say 'bout this, Renaldy? And I don't want to hear no smart-ass comments either. I ain't my nephew."

"Wait a fuckin' minute, I don't work for the DEA or FBI. I don't have access to any of these organizations. I'm a narcotics detective—I know what's going on in my jurisdiction. I'm a city employee, not a government civil servant!"

"Whatever, white boy," Kane responded. "You still a fuckin' cop, and she was a cop. I see a connection there."

"Ray, you need to get your nephew under control. His mouth is gonna get him in trouble!"

"Don't tell me what I need to do, cop. He's right—I am paying you to know everything about everything, no fuckin' excuses!" Ray jabbed a large, stiff finger into Renaldy's forehead.

"Everybody look at this piece of shit laying dead on the floor. Unless you want to end up just like her, you will keep your fuckin' mouth shut. Did anybody see shit?" Raymond hovered over Neecy as if to make it clear he was the predator and she had been the prey.

Everybody shook his or her head no at the same time. They all kept their heads and eyes low. Working for Ray had taught them that they had better not open their

K. Roland Williams

mouths under any circumstances. However, Raymond James wanted to be sure. He would take no chances with his freedom. He stepped in among the group of club employees silently.

He gave a sinister smile that the devil himself wouldn't trust and spoke calmly. Looking at Renaldy and Kane, then back at his staff, he said, "I need a volunteer. Who wants to be my employee of the month?"

fifteen

Antoinette stepped out of the shower to find Victor standing there with his arms behind his back waiting for her. He stared at her with a look that was more curiosity than anger. She was startled and covered her body automatically as if Victor were a stranger from the street standing in her bathroom.

"What the fuck, Victor? I can't have any privacy in the house either?"

"What the fuck happened to you today? It's almost twelve o'clock, and here you are strolling in singing and smelling like some other nigga!" Victor stepped up close to his wife and puffed up as if he would slap her. She didn't budge; she had enough of his shit to last a lifetime.

"Smelling like some fuckin' nigga? Victor, are you crazy? If you want to hit me, then hit me, nigga ... what you waiting on? But you don't know what the hell you're talking about, do you?"

She dropped her arms to expose her naked, vulnera-

K. Roland Williams

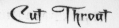
ble body and stepped close to Victor, waiting for him to strike her.

"Toni, I'm warning you ..."

"Warning me? Victor, I am warning you! The very next time you even act like you might hit me it better be to kill me 'cause your threatening days are over! And tracing my calls, having me followed ... all of your fucked up paranoia is not my problem—it's yours. If you can't trust me, then this marriage is over, and I'm not leaving this relationship empty-handed! I put too much of myself into this." She grabbed her towel and covered her still-wet body with it. Tears welled up in her eyes as Victor looked on silently. The panties he held in his tightly balled fist, the panties that he thought he would use as evidence against his wife, didn't seem valid anymore. He crumpled them into a ball and slid them into his pocket, thinking that maybe he had made a mistake.

"Toni, I'm sorry, I thought you were ..."

"You thought I was out fuckin' some other nigga, right? You have a problem, Victor. You don't trust anybody, not even your own wife. I know that the way we hooked up was fucked up, but why you constantly punishing me for that shit? We were both there in the beginning. It took both you and me to fuck Ray over, and it seems as if you think because I left him and cheated on him with you, I would do the same to you. That shit is not fair, Vic!"

"Look, like I said, Ricky saw you out with that Quincy

K. Roland Williams

character and the next thing I know he said you left with him. Explain that to me." Victor looked into his wife's eyes and waited for her response. He thought he knew when she was telling a lie. She would twist a lock of her hair subconsciously. Like a poker player calling a bluff, he could usually detect some hint of her untruth.

Toni did not twist her hair nor did she give her husband any indication that she was telling anything but the truth. She stood there, looked at him squarely in the eye and said, "The only person that I have fucked in the past several years has been *you*, Victor. Can you say the same thing?"

Victor waited and thought about the statement and the question, still looking Antoinette in her eye.

"I'm sorry, sweetie. That nigga told me you were hugged up wit' that other nigga, but I guess he was wrong and thought he saw something, huh?"

"I guess so, Victor. You need to go and slap his ass around."

A'ight, I was wrong … I am sorry. I'll let you get back to your *privacy*."

"Yeah, you do that," Toni said, feeling empowered and a bit surprised that her husband gave up so easily. *Am I turning into an expert liar like Victor?* she wondered as he left the massive shower and closed the door behind him.

Toni took a deep breath, composed herself and wiped her image into the steam-covered mirror. She stood

K. Roland Williams

there and took her breasts and curves in. Her beautiful cocoa complexion glistened in the recessed lighting of the grand marble shower.

She reached up and ran her fingers into a lock of damp hair and twisted the strands tightly, smiling. "Shit, Victor should be proud. I can lie with the best of them. I learned from the best."

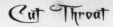
sixteen

Red and blue flashing lights illuminated the exterior of The Melody Room, making it perfectly clear that it was officially the scene of a crime. Bright strips of yellow police tape blocked the now-crowded entrance to the club's front door. Police, both uniformed and plain-clothed, walked back and forth, collecting evidence, taking pictures and questioning possible witnesses, though no one outside had seen a thing.

"I was first on the scene, closest homicide detective in the area." Renaldy smirked confidently at the two curious special agents as he glanced down at his small notebook. "Mr. James was up in his office when he heard two shots ring out. He then came downstairs to investigate and found this mess." Renaldy pointed down to the floor where two bodies outlined in white tape still lay, an uneven pool of dark blood coagulating under each.

"So let me get this right." The short agent cut his eyes narrowly, scrutinizing Renaldy's story. "You are telling

K. Roland Williams

me that you happened to be around the corner when you heard the call go through dispatch at 7:50?" The FBI agent glanced down at his own notebook. "Excuse me, 7:45."

"That's correct, Agent Griffith." Renaldy tried to stay cool, calm and collected despite the fact that his heart was going a mile a minute and his palms were as sweaty as a pimp caught up in a church service.

Agent Griffith continued to grill Renaldy and Ray as other detectives questioned the club employees. Raymond made sure to promise the employees a healthy financial contribution for them all to stay silent. He also promised a slow and agonizing death to any who ran their mouth or deviated from the last-minute plan that Renaldy and Ray devised.

Reginald Tate, a club employee, lay as still as a door knob on the floor, both eyes staring straight up to the ceiling as if in prayer to Jesus. Reggie occupied the second pool of blood across from Neecy, whose picture was being taken by a crime scene investigator.

Reggie's body had taken the place of Kane's, and the scene had been expertly set up by Renaldy to look as if Reggie and Neecy had shot each other in a horrible confrontation that no one seemed to know anything about. All the club's employees stuck to the same story, and it was the consensus of all who had watched the scene that Neecy and Reggie briefly argued, Neecy pulled her gun and Reggie pulled his own, then they both shot each other simultaneously, killing each other instantly.

The investigator snapped pictures of the scene and the coroner eventually arrived to remove the bodies.

"What do you think is really going on here?" one agent said to the other after pulling him to the side and out of earshot of anyone else.

"I'm not sure yet, but I do feel confident that there is a cover-up of some sort here. Diana was a competent, seasoned agent. She would not have gotten involved in some sort of dispute that might compromise her cover and get her killed in the process.

"I checked the body and her purse, and I haven't found her recorder and transmitter for the wire she was supposed to be wearing."

"She may not have had it on her at the time."

"Don't worry," the second agent said coldly while looking around the room. "We'll get to the bottom of this shit. She was one of us and whatever it takes, we *will* find out what happened here. I want you to start pulling information on every person in here—check every data-base we have. I'm more than positive that we'll find some interesting shit on the owner and the cop. Make sure to contact local internal affairs and see if this Renaldy character has any red flags on him. I won't be surprised if he does."

Raymond looked from across the room as the coroner's office technician nonchalantly zipped the thick, black, latex body bag over Reggie Tate's lifeless corpse.

K. Roland Williams

Reggie's eyes were still partially open, blank, cold and still confused, even in death.

"Thanks for volunteering, Reggie, I appreciate your help." Raymond said to himself and then smiled, glancing over at Renaldy next to the two FBI agents. "You're next on my shitlist, motherfucker, you're next."

Raymond flipped open his cell phone and dialed a number. "How's your shoulder, nephew?" he said in a thin whisper.

"I'll live," Kane said in a guttural grunt as the pain ripped into his shoulder and neck. The bullet hole still leaked a now-heavy stream of blood despite the makeshift bandage that covered it, out of sight under his jacket.

"Did you call the doctor I told you to call?"

"Yeah, we on our way there now so he can sew me back up."

"Look, after you see the doc, you and your crew hit the street and find Quincy's ass. I know you in pain but this takes priority. Both our lives are on the line. I don't know what's on the tape that bitch made, but Quincy has it. He may be on his way to the cops right now for all I know. I need you to find him—bring his ass to me one way or the other. He can't give anybody that wire or it's both our asses. Do you understand me?"

"Yeah, I understand. I can finally bust a cap in his bitch ass." Kane was thinking that this was all Raymond's sloppy-ass fault, running his mouth and shit the way he had been.

"Whatever, just get all of the tapes and the wire *first*. I don't care how you get it, but you have to get the wire first. Don't fuck this up, or it will be your ass getting zipped up in a body bag, family or not! Oh, and Quincy has a gun, so be careful."

Δ Δ Δ Δ

Quincy drove through the streets of southeast D.C. nervously, under torrential rainfall. Not sure what his next step should be, he played the events through his head like a movie, waiting to get a return call from Xavier.

Xavier, he thought to himself. He knew they had their issues, but he was the only nigga who was close to his location. The other band members were way across town and Q wanted to dump the car and lay low sooner rather than later. The more he drove, the greater the chance the cops would pinpoint Renaldy's stolen police car. *Fuck*, Q thought, *of all the times to be having a problem wit' this nigga.* If Ray found him he was a dead man for sure. He could have called one of his many girlfriends, but they would ask way too many questions.

Xavier would be able to supply Quincy with a dry sanctuary and precious time to think. A few hours of quiet would be enough time for Quincy to get his head right and formulate a decent plan.

K. Roland Williams

Quincy pulled over to take a leak. He ran under the tattered awning of a dilapidated building. An old Chinese restaurant stood there silently in the dark recess of the building; the Chinese characters represented the name of the abandoned restaurant fading into nothing on the broken wall amidst the graffiti gang tags. The stench of urine and the sharp crunch of broken crack vials under foot distracted him from the thought of Neecy's fading eyes. Each thought of her plagued his mind and made him both sad and angry for revenge.

"What did she say her real name was again? Diana Lawson?" Her last words echoed in his head and played in a repeating loop. Shit, the times that they had gone out had been nice. Quincy tripped on the idea that she had been a cop the entire time that they had dated.

He tried to call his boy again, but the line came up busy. "Shit, this nigga on the phone runnin' his mouth. Why won't his cheap ass get a fuckin' two-way line?" Q dialed his number again, and this time it rang.

"Where you at?" finally came through the other end of Quincy's receiver. Clearly, Xavier still had caller ID.

"Finally. Look, Xavier, I don't want to argue with you about none of this band shit right now. I don't know how much life the battery on my cell phone has, so I got to get to the point. I can't say much right now, but I need to talk to you. I got to have a place to think for a minute."

"Look, I got your message a minute ago. No problem, you know you can come here if you need to. Where are you now?" Xavier sounded more anxious than concerned about his best friend's well-being.

"I appreciate that, bruh," Quincy said, sliding deeper into the darkness of the building's doorway as the flash of lights from an oncoming car pointed his way, illuminating the façade of the condemned structure.

"Fuck all the bullshit and drama before, you know you're welcome at my crib anytime you want. But what's going on? Why can't you go home? What the fuck happened at the club?"

"Damn, nigga, I said I would explain it to you soon enough!" Quincy caught his temper and evened his tone. "Look, man, I'll be there in about two hours. I'll explain everything then."

"You sure you straight? Why is it gonna take you two hours, you can't get here sooner?"

"It's all good, I need to take my time with this and think about some things. Two hours ... see you then."

"A'ight, bro, I'll see you in a few hours."

"Holla." Quincy pressed the end call on his cell phone and pulled up the collar on his blood-soaked, rain-drenched shirt and hauled himself out from under the piss-filled doorway and back to the stolen police car.

Δ Δ Δ Δ

"Yo, Kane, you were right," Xavier said. "He did call me and he's on his way over right now to my house. You

K. Roland Williams

might want to send your peoples over here to intercept his ass. He said he would be here in two hours." Xavier showed no sign of concern over the betrayal of his so-called friend. In fact, his tone was a cold expression of his contempt for his boy Quincy. Quincy had taken over his band, the limelight and the chance of Xavier ever being the star of the show. With Q out of the picture, he would be the boss.

"He said he would be there in two hours, huh? I'll be there in one and a half with my boys. Don't fuck this up or it will be *your* head that I bring back to Ray on a silver fuckin' platter, not Quincy's—ya heard me?"

"Don't worry, Kane, he'll be here. Tell Raymond that I'll be taking over the band from today on."

"Whatever, Xavier, whatever."

Δ Δ Δ Δ

Quincy slowed the car to a stand still. He wasn't sure why he felt that strange pang in his stomach, the kind of feeling that comes to some folks right before something bad was about to happen. Something about Xavier's tone did not quite sit right with Quincy. Xavier was dis-tant, and it almost seemed as if he were expecting Quincy's call. Quincy sped the car up now and decided to make his way to X's house sooner rather than later. If he hurried, he could get across the bridge and to Xavier's crib in about fifteen minutes.

K. Roland Williams

Quincy's mind raced, and he thought to himself, *My early arrival will give me a chance to scope things out just in case there is going to be some bullshit.* He took the back way west on Jessup Street and then made a right on Grant, right around the corner from his boy Xavier's crib.

When he arrived around the corner, he parked the cruiser out of sight and made his way around the back, quietly making sure not to rattle trashcans or disturb neighbors who looked for any excuse to put their nose in business that didn't belong to them. Quincy lay back in the cut, almost swallowed up by the two condemned buildings that were perched on either side of him. The rain finally slowed to a sporadic drizzle, but it was still an annoyance to the water-logged Quincy. "This is bullshit," Quincy mumbled to himself, fighting back the urge to sneeze. *Great, that is all I need now ... a cold. Not like I'll be singing anywhere or anytime soon.*

Quincy positioned himself between the apartment buildings in the dark directly across the street from Xavier's house. He crouched low next to a stinking trashcan and allowed his eyes to adjust to the dark. The rain reluctantly slowed to a warm drizzle and eventually stopped altogether. The yellow streetlights outside of X's apartment sufficiently illuminated the old brick row house and X's three series Bimmer that sat outside in front. New chrome rims glistened wet and bright in the light.

"New rims and a new, expensive-ass watch, Xavier

K. Roland Williams

has definitely had a come-up lately." Quincy wiped the rain from his wet hair and flicked it away. Q knew that his boy wasn't telling him everything, and the longer he sat there in that dark, stinking hole between the buildings, the clearer it became that something more was going on. Xavier had been too cold lately, too fucking cynical. It wasn't his style.

A white SUV slowly pulled up in front of X's place, blocking Quincy's view of the front of the building. The tinted windows made it impossible to see the driver or the passengers, but Quincy did count the six pair of Timberland boots that hit the ground from the passenger's side. A voice rang out in the dark, clearly giving instructions to the driver to take the truck around to the back of the building and park it in the alleyway.

The Expedition pulled away to reveal Kane and three of his thugs. The men looked around briefly and said a few things to each other under their breath. The three men walked up to the front door and rang the doorbell. Kane followed them but stopped short of the stoop and turned to glare at the dark slit across the street where Quincy sat perched. Q stopped breathing for a second and tried to disappear into the pitch black between the buildings. Q, his eyes now adjusted to the lack of light, could see Kane, but Kane saw nothing but looming shadows. Kane squinted from across the street and thought better of investigating further. He turned and entered the now-open door of Xavier's apartment, clos-

K. Roland Williams

ing the door behind him.

"That motherfucker!" Quincy was heated, though he wasn't surprised at all. All Q's speculation was now fact. His boy of fifteen years had set him up—and good.

A large brown rat scurried along the wall next to Quincy and out beyond the safety of the darkness into the night. Quincy barely noticed. He stood on sore, tight legs and fought back the desire to scream when a cramp tore through his left calf. He reached for the almost-lifeless cell phone and dialed Xavier's home number.

"Yo, X, I'm still coming, but I'm going to be a little later than I thought."

"Err ahh, a'ight ... well, hurry up, man, I'm getting sleepy as hell and I want to lay my ass down."

"Like I said, I'm en route. Hey, I wanted to ask you though ... is everything still cool between us?"

"What do you mean ... cool?" Xavier hesitated, apparently caught off-guard with the query. "Why wouldn't it be? We go back too fuckin' far, homey." X forced a smile so that the lie would sound genuine and not like the bullshit he was now spitting.

"Good to know, X, I was worried that our friendship was slippin'. You know, you taking over the band and all that shit. The argument the other day ..."

"Don't trip, just get here and we'll get everything squared away and out in the open ... just get here."

Quincy hung up, pulled Renaldy's gun from his waistband and moved around to the back of the buildings. He

K. Roland Williams

silently moved close to where the truck had been parked. He watched intently for the man who had driven the truck, which sat next to a set of dumpsters. No one was in sight, just a cat that jumped up into the dumpster's ledge and disappeared inside.

Q moved to the truck, trying to get a better view of the house and what Kane and his muscle were doing inside. Before Quincy could really see anything, a man came from behind the building, zipping his jeans up after taking a piss. It was one of Kane's hoods, and he startled Quincy. The man reached into his waistline and pulled a gun, yelling for Quincy to stop and get away from the truck and for Kane and the rest of his crew to come out of Xavier's house. Quincy didn't budge and within seconds, Quincy heard the first three shots ring out, hitting the side of the truck in rapid succession. The forty-five caliber rounds hit with enough power to rock the truck.

Quincy ducked into the truck, low and hard below the dashboard, trying to dip away from the flying bullets. He dropped Renaldy's gun on the floor. The keys were still in the ignition—*God must be watching*, Quincy thought. He started the truck and it growled to life. He slammed his foot on the gas, trying to maneuver the large SUV around the dumpster and piles of trash, but instead smashed head-on into the dumpster, throwing him forward. He knew the game would end there if he couldn't get the vehicle moving again quickly. Two more shots rang out as the men closed the distance between

K. Roland Williams

the building and Quincy. The last round struck the rear passenger window and the glass exploded like a bomb had gone off.

Reaching for the gun on the floorboard of the passenger side, Quincy stretched hard toward the weapon. Footsteps surrounded the truck, and Quincy could hear the metallic *click clack* of weapons being prepared to fire, clips being slid into place and slides being cocked back, ready for action.

Kane's voice was clear as a bell. "Quincy, is that you?" Kane yelled out. "I knew I felt something wasn't right. You are a hell of a lot smarter than you look, ma'-fucka. Listen to me, you can get out of this, you know. All you have to do is come out of there real easy like—no one is gonna get shot." Kane nodded to a tall man with a black and gold Pittsburgh throwback to move in closer to the truck.

"Fuck you, muthafucker, come in here and get me out!" Quincy yelled back while stretching his arm out for the gun, reaching it this time.

"Fuck this, Trey, take those fuckin' tires out. He won't get far on four fuckin' flats."

Before the man could fire his weapon, Quincy, with adrenaline coursing wildly through his veins, pointed the heavy weapon at the closest man and squeezed the trigger. Nothing happened.

"Fucking safety is still on." He thumbed the small black lever until he saw the red dot indicating the gun

K. Roland Williams

was hot, and he squeezed the trigger again. This time it exploded in his hand. The recoil shook his arm and shoulder, kicking the gun up from the blast. The loudness of the weapon was deafening, but Quincy fired several more times, not sure if he hit anyone but sure that all the niggaz trying to surround the truck were now scattering like bitches in all directions.

He threw the gun into the passenger seat, turned the wheel on the truck hard to the right and slammed the truck into the dumpster again, pushing it out of his way. He sideswiped several more trashcans and dumpsters in his haste to exit the alley. As he drove out past the rear of X's house, Quincy could see Xavier laid out on his back porch, arms wide like a snow angel, apparently hit by a stray bullet. He wasn't moving, but Quincy didn't have time to stop. He knew he may have shot Xavier in the short exchange of gunfire with Kane and his boys, but Quincy didn't feel remorse at that moment—just anger.

The odor of gun smoke was heavy and pungent in the air. Quincy's head was swimming with adrenaline and fear, but he felt surprisingly lucid and satisfied. He felt good with the notion that he had fought back. It would only be a matter of time before Kane and his boys jumped into Xavier's car, so he had to put some serious distance between him and the criminals.

Quincy swerved and maneuvered through the side streets, trying to avoid the police by any means necessary. The wind whipped through the broken window of the truck as Q grabbed for his mobile in his pocket. Scrolling through the menu as he drove, he chose a number, hit the send button and waited.

"Hello." The voice on the other end was soft and calm. The exact opposite of everything that surrounded Quincy at the moment.

"Antoinette, I need your help, I need to meet with you now. There is no one else I can trust ... I just got into a fucking gun fight with ..."

"Calm down, Quincy, tell me where you want to meet, and I will be there." Antoinette looked over to her husband's side of the bed. He was, of course, nowhere to be found.

"Meet me at the Starbucks where we met to go over the contract. Say in about twenty minutes. I'm depending on you."

Trusting this woman he barely knew was a crazy-ass move, but the truth was, he had nowhere else to turn.

"You know I'll be there. Are you okay?" Her voice was full of concern as she wiped the sleep from her eyes.

"I will be when I see you. See you soon," Quincy said and disconnected the call.

Another risk, another fuckin' unknown. The last few days had been full of them. Q knew he was pushing it and that his luck would more than likely run out soon, but he had to keep it moving. He doubled back to where he had dumped the police car, switched the cruiser's

K. Roland Williams

plates with the truck's plates and sped off. Exhausted, he gathered his courage and drove quickly to meet Antoinette Sweet.

Δ Δ Δ Δ

Renaldy's phone rang loudly and startled him from his nap while he sat in a new Crown Vic outside of the precinct, waiting to hear from Kane. The questioning from the Feds had certainly shaken him up, and he knew that his relationship with Raymond had gotten out of control. Raymond killing the Fed and that boy at the club was a bad, bad move and the evidence would not add up. He knew that it was just a matter of time before it came back to bite him in the ass. Besides that, Raymond had looked at him differently tonight.

It scared the shit out him. Renaldy had been in many, many tight spots in his career, more than he was willing to admit, but that look from Raymond meant that he would eventually kill Renaldy—he simply knew too much. Renaldy knew about the money, several bodies and the drug connects.

Shit, I would want to shut me up, too, if I were him, Renaldy thought.

The mobile rang again, waking Renaldy from his day-dream.

"Yeah, Renaldy here."

Kane responded with an equally rash voice. "We

have a serious problem. A problem that my uncle does-n't need to know about!"

"I'm listening," Renaldy said.

"Quincy just stole one of my trucks and took off." The arrogant growl usually present in his voice was gone, the embarrassment of the shoot out and the stolen truck now almost too much for Kane to bear.

"What, you had him, and let him get away? Tell me you at least got the wire from him. Please tell me you got it!"

"No, I didn't get the wire. Like I said, we had him cornered. He stole my truck and got away!"

"Okay, now what do you want *me* to do about that?"

"I need you to call in a few of your cop friends to help us look for this nigga, that's what I want you to do. I know you have some people you can trust, right?"

Kane sounded desperate, and he was clearly in a serious bind and Renaldy sensed the weakness in his voice.

"I'll give you a description of the truck, and you can give your boys an *all points*. Not the entire force, just a handful of cops you can trust. Cops and trust—I never thought I would use those two words together in a sentence," Kane said. "But we need to find his bama ass!"

Renaldy thought he would push the young black man's buttons. "Let me see if I get this straight. You want me to use my resources to get your ass out of a bad situation, so that your uncle and boss don't find out just

K. Roland Williams

how bad your black ass fucked up!" Renaldy laughed aloud.

"Listen you fat, white, pasty motherfucka, don't get it twisted. This shit ain't all fallin' on my shoulders, not by a fuckin' long shot!" Kane gathered his bravado slowly but surely.

"Why do you think I give a rat's ass about your problems?"

"Well, for one thing, if you help me find Quincy before my uncle finds out about our little ... incident, I'll make sure you get back into his good graces."

"I didn't know that I was on his bad side." Renaldy hesitated, waiting for the response from Kane that he knew was coming.

"Shit, cop, we already dug the fuckin' hole that you're gonna be buried in. All we need are a few bags of lime and it's a done deal for you. How's that for a fuckin' reason?"

Renaldy's breathing trailed off into what sounded like a slight gasp. He considered his options for a brief moment, finally coming to the only conclusion that made sense. "Give me the description of this fucking truck you're talking about." Renaldy sighed.

"Well, this is what we need to do," Kane said.

Δ Δ Δ Δ

After leaving the police cruiser around the corner

from the Starbucks, Q had noticed that his own car, which he'd left earlier, was still there, but they were sure to be looking for it by now. He had been so exhausted that when Toni pulled up in her Benz he fell into the car, almost unconscious, and dropped into an immediate sleep as if he had been drugged.

Quincy woke to find himself sitting in Antoinette's empty car in a dark parking garage. His head cloudy with sleep, he instinctively reached for the nine millimeter that was stuck down into the waistband of his jeans. The gun was still where he had left it, and the weight of the thing, though a foreign object to Quincy, was a reassuring presence.

Quincy looked down at his Sean John jeans and ruined shirt, wondering how he would be able to walk into any door without drawing serious attention to himself. Anyone who saw him would have to think he just murdered a house full of folks. The blood on his clothes was so thick that it made his pants stiff like some strange red starch.

Removing himself from the car, he focused on the sign that hung from the exterior of the parking garage, visible through the columns of the parking structure. "Four Seasons Resort and Spa" was what the sign read. Apparently, Antoinette had plans for Quincy, a place where he could relax and get his head right, maybe hang out until Monday morning when he could finally get a chance to talk to Neecy's superiors at the FBI.

K. Roland Williams

Quincy heard Antoinette's heels clacking against the concrete long before he could see her. A few seconds later, she came around the corner with a plush white robe folded across her left arm, a key in her right hand and a gentle smile on her face.

"Quincy, put this on and cover up all of that blood, I don't want these white folks up in here calling the cops 'cause you looking like a serial killer. You need to hurry up and tell me what's going on."

"Don't worry, I will as soon as I get a nice, hot shower and some food into my stomach." Quincy slid the plush white robe on and covered his blood-soaked clothing.

"I feel like a nut walking through the garage with a robe on," Quincy said.

"Better the robe on than off, trust me. We'll take the garage elevator to the lobby and then another to our floor, and hopefully, if we are lucky, no one will see us at this hour. Everyone should be asleep anyway."

Quincy and Antoinette entered the lobby-level elevator and exited on the fourteenth floor, made a left and stopped at room 1408. Antoinette slid the key card into the slot and the door unlocked with a green light and quiet beeping sound.

"A little easier than your door at home, huh, Quincy?" she said with a smile.

"No doubt," Quincy responded.

"All right, Quincy, look ... I plan to run and find some-

K. Roland Williams

where to get us something to eat, and while I am gone, you can get cleaned up. I should be back in under an hour, okay?"

"I really appreciate what you're doing for me, Toni. I know you're taking a risk helping me."

"Well, I don't know how much of a risk I'm taking yet, but you can clear that up when I get back. Besides, I have to make sure I take care of my number one investment."

"No, I'm serious, I do appreciate it." He raised her chin up gently with his hand and looked sincerely into her brown eyes.

She pulled away from Quincy. "And so am I. You are an investment. Don't worry, you'll be paying for this room eventually anyway, it'll come off of your end when you start producing some revenue." Antoinette laughed aloud and pushed Quincy's shoulder.

"You are a trip, girl."

"No, Quincy, it's just business, nothing personal. I'm sure you've heard that many times before."

"Yeah, fucking around with Ray at the club, you hear it on the regular."

The second Quincy mentioned Raymond, Antoinette made a beeline for the door of the plush hotel room. "See you in a little while, Quincy," she said. "Don't forget to wash all of the good parts. Oh yeah, I made arrangements with the hotel concierge to get you some clean clothes, too." She smiled and walked out of the room.

K. Roland Williams

seventeen

"Okay, here's the deal." Renaldy stopped for a second to light his cigarette. He inhaled deeply, almost enough to burn the tobacco and paper down to the butt.

Looking out over the small group of off-duty, plain-clothes cops, he gave a false background of the target, along with pictures, and a made up case that had been scribbled down on a legal pad and copied a few times. Quincy Underwood was now officially a wanted felon—armed, dangerous and clearly capable of anything—or at least that's what had been fabricated about him.

The cops, all associates of Renaldy, either owed him a favor or were hungry to bust heads, preferably black heads. The four men present in the room were the kind of cops who made all good cops look bad, the kind of cops who would shoot to kill, even if it was not warranted or necessary. Somewhere along the line they had all shared a sin or two. Either beating a man to death, shooting and killing an unarmed man or planting drugs

K. Roland Williams

on an assailant that they wanted to falsely build a case on. Most of the victims had been African American or Hispanic males.

Renaldy had put together a dossier of his target, and this special operation had top priority written all over it. All the cops there were manipulative, dangerous and clearly motivated by money—all good characteristics considering the kind of work that was needed that night. Some would call the room full of police bad cops, others would call them opportunists, but that night they were mercenaries.

"Baptiste, O'Conner, Figaro, Graham, I appreciate your coming out." Renaldy donned a fake smile and greeted the dirty cops. Two were detectives like Renaldy, two beat cops known for their heavy-handed approach to crime in the streets.

"Let's get right to it, Renaldy, tell us what we have to do to get this twenty grand."

"It's twenty grand total, five thousand a piece." Renaldy clarified the financial particulars as one of the cops got up and quietly closed the door to the room.

"I get the impression," O'Conner said, "this is a classified operation?"

"Correct, we have to limit our communication to *these* throw-away cell phones," he held up a bag of pirated cells provided by Raymond, "and/or special frequencies on the radios."

Renaldy pulled out an eight-by-ten glossy picture of

K. Roland Williams

Quincy and showed it to the men, holding it up high for all to see. In addition, he provided the license plate number of Antoinette Sweet's Mercedes and her physical description. He remembered the plate number from picking Quincy up at his apartment, and there would be a good chance that they may be together. The plate read *Cut Throat*; it should be easy enough to spot.

"These two will be our targets and the catch of the day." Renaldy passed copies of the same picture of Quincy to all the men. "This man is clearly African American, six foot even, 220 pounds, medium to muscular build and is considered armed and dangerous. He is wanted for the murder of an FBI agent earlier tonight and needs to be picked up within the next few hours—before Monday morning."

"Why before Monday morning?" O'Conner asked.

"Because that's the timeline that the Feds have given us. Consider this a joint venture with the FBI. Due to its sensitive nature, 'discretion' is the word of the day. Keep it inside of these four walls only!"

Renaldy lit up another cigarette and gave his degenerate group of cops the remaining information, which was passed around and studied, each man taking in all of the available info on their target—his address, addresses of family and friends, hangout locations.

"An additional two grand over the five for the man who actually brings him in to me." Renaldy blew smoke from the corner of his mouth and waited for additional questions from the men.

"Another nigger off of the street is a great day. Shit, I would do this for nothing on a regular day, but seeming as I want the down payment for my boat, what the hell—I'm in."

"Good, I'm glad you intend on blessing us with your fuckin' presence."

The men gathered the folders and discussed a few details briefly before hitting the streets separately. Renaldy knew that several points of several arrows would be more successful than the point of his one spear.

"Last thing before you guys start the search-and-destroy mission, if you find him, you have to get the tape and wire from him before we do anything else. And the woman is not to be touched!"

"I don't see how we can find him in such a short period of time," one of the cops said, careful not to yell too loud.

"Antoinette Sweet has a LoJack system on her car. I have a call in and I'm waiting on a response from their office. They should be tracking her vehicle now. As soon as I can get her car triangulated, I'll feed the info to you ... this is key to this being a success. Once you see him, you call everyone and we all converge at the same time, to tighten the noose." All the men laughed at the implications of Renaldy's last comment and looked at each other in a silent racial agreement. Renaldy looked out at

K. Roland Williams

the men and reiterated the importance of getting the wire, then dismissed the anxious men who pushed away from the table and dispersed to find Quincy Underwood at all costs.

Δ Δ Δ Δ

Quincy stood under the surge of steaming water, allowing it to wash away his problems for the moment. He watched the last remnants of the woman he knew as Neecy circle and wash down the shower's drain in a blood-red whirlpool. He grieved for the woman still, and he couldn't help but think that he had something to do with the fucked up way it all ended for her.

"If I hadn't been fuckin' wit' that dirty motherfucka Kane ..." Q punched the tiled wall of the shower, almost breaking his right fist. He pulled his hand back in pain.

"Time to start playing this game the right fuckin' way," Q said to himself. "I've been soft up till now. I got to harden up, take it back to the projects where I'm from, I ain't no fuckin' mark-ass coward! If I don't do it for nobody else, I'll do it for you, Neecy ... Diana, if that was even your real name, I'll do it for you."

Q washed every inch of his body from the crown of his head to the balls of his still-sore feet. At any rate, Q felt a new surge of energy, the shower reviving his instinctual desire to get through his trying situation. He wouldn't let this depress him to the point of quitting and

K. Roland Williams

giving up his life and future.

He was startled by the sound of the bathroom door opening. Quincy looked through the foggy etched glass of the shower door and saw a form moving toward the door quickly through the steam. The gun might as well have been a million miles away on the sink. Before Q could react, the door opened quickly and Antoinette stood there in all of her naked glory, with nothing on but a very sly grin.

Antoinette stood there for a brief second, looking Quincy up and down. Her eyes gravitated to his flaccid dick, counting the inches it would swell right before her eyes the moment she got her hands around it.

Q could see Antoinette staring and he stared at her as well. Her nipples were erect, and the steam from the shower began to accumulate on her body until it glistened like dew on a black rose.

"You gonna just stand there with yo' fine ass?" Quincy extended his hand and Antoinette couldn't help but be reminded of Billy Dee Williams and Diana Ross in *"Lady Sings the Blues."* "You gonna let my hand fall off?"

That ol'-school-ass movie flashed and played briefly in her head. She took Q's hand and entered the steamy hotel shower.

K. Roland Williams

eighteen

"Antoinette Sweet's Mercedes was tracked in Georgetown a few minutes ago from the LoJack people. They're having problems with their system, so the information is going in and out." The cop spoke into his radio and described what his informant had just recently described to him. Renaldy was pleased as pie to hear that his plan was working already. It had only been a little over an hour and they were already getting results.

Ten eyes are better than two, Renaldy thought to himself. Kane and his bunch of unprofessional cut-throats were out pounding the pavement and looking for Quincy as well, but the chances that the untrained thugs would find anything were slim to none. "Those fuckin' porch monkeys couldn't find their own cocks if they were in their hands and they were having a pissing contest, let alone one man in a city as large as D.C." Renaldy hadn't even told Kane about finding out about the LoJack on Antoinette's Benz. He didn't want Kane and his boys in the way, so he let them drive around and do things the hard way.

"All right, keep your eyes peeled and start to close the noose at a two mile radius. As soon as we get the next report from the LoJack folks we should have an exact location within a few hundred feet, so just stand by."

Δ Δ Δ Δ

Antoinette moved slowly into Quincy's strong, welcoming arms. The hot water of the shower cascaded over their naked bodies and pooled between the places where her breasts and his muscular chest came together.

Usually, getting her hair wet would be a no-no unless she was in the shampoo bowl at her girl Mia's salon in Bethesda, but today it didn't even matter. What *did* matter was moving on to step two of her plan to seduce and control Quincy. Getting him to do her bidding would require a combination of her sweet pussy and Q's desire for fame. Antoinette never underestimated a man's greed or the power of a woman's pussy.

Their lips and tongues met as they kissed deeply and passionately. Their pelvises moved together to a silent orchestra, the only real music playing was the pelting rhythm of the waterfall shower. Q turned Antoinette around and slid his naked body slowly up and down against her wet ass. He cupped both of her breasts, gen-

K. Roland Williams

tly at first, and then more firmly, until her nipples stood erect and her pussy ached for his dick.

He made sure not to miss her favorite spots—her ear-lobes, shoulders and the nape of her neck. They were all kissed and licked attentively. Q's tongue was skillful and Antoinette thought she might come just by the touching and deep kissing. She turned to him and moved down, kissing and sucking his nipples, going lower as she licked her way down across his flat, washboard stom-ach, and eventually to his now fully erect manhood.

Antoinette kissed Q's thighs and started to tease the tip of his dick with her darting tongue. She flicked her tongue against the sensitive spot just below the head of his penis, and Q extended both arms out to brace him-self against the shower. Antoinette took him into her mouth all the way and began to slide his dick in and out of her throat. Her technique was the shit and Q groaned, moving his hips to the beat that she created.

Antoinette could feel Q's body movement shift into overdrive, which meant he was gearing up to come. She instinctively slowed the pace to make sure he didn't shoot his nut too soon. She wanted to milk him longer and make his orgasm that much more powerful. She knew a satisfied man would be a more agreeable man, so she pulled her mouth off of his shaft and moved back up to his nipples.

Before she knew it, Quincy had her up against the cold marble of the shower wall, his mouth all over her breasts. He pulled her leg up and slid his hard dick up and down her clit, slow at first and then faster with an unheard rhythm that guided him and his movements.

Antoinette groaned in response to his hardness against her soft, wet pussy. She could feel herself relaxing and giving in to his desire. She thought that under different circumstances this man could be her full time lover—he had fuckin' skills.

Quincy dropped down on his knee and gently caressed her throbbing clit with his finger and opened her lips wide with both of his thumbs—her pussy whispered to him to taste her. He dove in deep with his tongue and she thought she would faint.

The sex went on for quite a while, long enough for them both to come two times each.

Δ Δ Δ Δ

Quincy rolled over and looked hard and long at Antoinette as she slept next to him on the bed. He drank in the smooth softness of her face. She was a beautiful woman even while she slept.

Quincy's intuition spoke to him as he watched Antoinette sleep deeply. He slowly swung around and carefully slipped off of the high double-pillow top mattress.

Toni's purse was on the table in the living room of the suite. The Louis Vuitton was already unzipped and her

K. Roland Williams

cell phone vibrated in the expensive handbag. Q's curiosity got the best of him—he reached inside the purse and removed the mobile, glancing back at the door to the bedroom, which was slightly cracked open.

The bedroom was quiet and still, Antoinette apparently still resting, unaware of Q's prying eyes. Q flipped up the phone's clamshell to see that several messages had been left and quite a few calls missed. Q thumbed through her phone's menu, looking at previous calls both made and received. He tried to do so quietly and carefully.

One number was familiar as hell. It took several seconds for the series of numbers to take shape in Q's still-foggy head, but they eventually did. The phone number was Xavier's.

"Do you have a fucking habit of going through a woman's purse?" Antoinette was only a few feet away from Quincy, catching him off-guard as he dropped the mobile back into the purse nonchalantly.

"No, I don't, but under the circumstances, I didn't want to use the hotel phone, and I didn't want to wake you, you were sleeping so soundly." Q tried to sound unaffected by her sneaking up and catching him.

"Hmmm, well," she replied, "the next time you need to use a phone, my phone ... ask, okay?"

"Of course, Toni." He smiled, trying not to give up the fact that he had just seen some super shady shit. He walked back into the bedroom without a glance back,

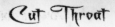

and his naked ass disappeared around the corner and into the luxurious bathroom of the suite.

Antoinette waited until she heard him close the door. She pulled the cell out and checked the missed calls and messages, then engaging her password—*cutthroat*—she shut the phone off altogether.

What the fuck is he looking for? she thought. *Time is ticking.*

Δ Δ Δ Δ

Quincy moved the pile of towels on the counter top, revealing the wire and receiver that he had escaped the club with along with the nine millimeter he'd taken from Renaldy. He fingered the small button on the wire to see how much life was still in the device. The small red light blinked on briefly and then switched to a bright green, indicating that it was operational. The microphone that dangled from the device was still intact and looked like it would work well enough, if Quincy needed it.

K. Roland Williams

n i n e t e e n

"Forgive me, Father, for I have sinned." Renaldy made an imaginary cross with his hand from chin to chest and side-to-side. "Yea though I walk through the valley of the shadow of death, I shall fear no evil—" Renaldy's radio crackled to life and interrupted his makeshift Sunday mass service. "Shit," he replied before responding to Baptiste, the beat cop born and raised in New Orleans and now serving his second year on the D.C. Metro.

Baptiste had been displaced when Katrina broke up the entire city of New Orleans, totally fucking up the police department in the Big Easy. "An on-duty cruiser just reported a truck all shot to shit not far from here. You think that has anything to do with your boy?"

"Naw, don't worry 'bout the truck. We're focused on the Mercedes," Renaldy responded. "We should hear something about the location of her car any second now, just sit tight. I need him found by daybreak and that gives you about ... six hours."

Renaldy looked down at the old Timex that his father had left him many years ago before he passed away. His father had also been a cop, but a clean cop, the kind of cop Renaldy had promised his dad he would become one day—a promise that he had broken.

∆ ∆ ∆ ∆

"Somehow I think this could come in handy," Quincy said to himself, studying the electronic gadget that he had gotten from Neecy.

The knock on the door shook Q out of his concentration. He slid the device next to the gun and covered them with the towel.

"Come in, Toni."

"Can we talk, Q?"

"Of course, what's up?"

Wasting no time, she asked, "How bad do you want this dream of yours?"

"It depends on what dream you're talking about."

"You know damn well what I'm talking about—your dream of being a star, a top of the chart artist, the whole nine."

"Antoinette, you know I want that to become a reality. It's all I ever wanted."

"Well, Q, the dream has come as close as it's going to get; you need to take a few steps toward it now. No, fuck that, you need to run full speed toward your dream now.

K. Roland Williams

If you want that dream, it's time to act like it."

Antoinette's soft face grew harder and more serious by the second. She slowly transformed right before Q's eyes into another woman altogether. The woman who he had just made love to was gone and had been replaced with a cold-hearted, scandalous bitch.

"I thought I already had the deal. What do I have to do to make this a reality?"

"I need a serious commitment from you now. I need to know that you're down for me *whatever* it takes to make this happen, whatever it takes."

Quincy looked puzzled by this strange change of character. Antoinette had clearly told him in previous meetings that this contract, despite what her husband might think or say, was a done deal. He would be Cut Throat's next R&B soloist.

"Antoinette, you need to get to the point." Quincy began dressing in the clean clothes she had arranged for him.

"Look, I am prepared to bring you in on this entire empire. I will give you 50 percent of Cut Throat Records. Fuck the record deal. Artists don't make money anyway, you know that. What I am offering is ownership beside me, running all of it together."

Q hesitated and gave Antoinette a perplexed look. "I don't think Victor would be too happy about that. What the fuck are you talking about, Toni?"

Antoinette grew tired and impatient with Quincy's

K. Roland Williams

naiveté and exploded.

"Are you really this dense? Don't you *want* to be rich, Q? You want to get out of the hood and have anything and everything you've ever dreamed about, right?" She moved closer to Q, trying to use her sexuality to sway him as she had earlier that night in the shower.

"I can make this happen for you." She grabbed his right hand, and laid it on her breasts, sliding his hand across her nipples. "Can't you imagine having this pussy anytime you want, with no hiding and sneaking around? We could fly to Spain for breakfast on our own private jet, fuck until we can barely walk and fly back the same night to fuck again in our own penthouse. That's the kind of money that I'm talking about, Quincy ... can you get with that?"

"It all sounds great, Toni," he said, snatching his hand away. "But the *only* way that's going to ever happen is over your husband's dead body. Let me ask you a question. How do you know Xavier, and why is his number in your mobile?"

She hesitated, collected her thoughts and smiled at Quincy as if to say the gig was up, she would come clean. "How do you think I came to pick you, Quincy? You think it was a coincidence that I ended up in Raymond's club after all that happened between Ray and me? It was your boy, Q—Xavier—who set that up."

"What the fuck are you talking about, Toni? Xavier set what up?"

K. Roland Williams

"Your partner, Xavier, and I met a while back at a function and we started talking about his music career. We stayed in touch for a while and I knew he could sing, but he wasn't the full package. He wasn't as good as you. I thought about giving him an opportunity, but eventually I changed my mind when I heard about you. One thing led to another, I shared a few personal things with him, and he implied that with you in the midst of this thing between Ray and Victor, he would be free to do what he wanted with the band. If the thing played out, you would be out of the picture entirely and he would sign with Cut Throat.

"Well, I didn't want you out of the picture. I want Victor out of the picture. If I could use you for that purpose then so be it. That was our deal. He gave me the idea in the first place. It was just a matter of getting close to you and bringing all of the parts together. It was a sloppy plan, I admit, but the fastest thing that I could come up with at the time."

"Let me see if I understand this correctly. You and my boy devised a plan to steal me away from Ray and the band to get Ray to go to war with Victor because I signed with Cut Throat? What if he would have just said fuck it and put X back in my spot as lead?"

"I know Raymond like the back of my hand. He would never have just let you go like that. It's the principle of the thing. Besides, you leaving to go to work for Victor in the music industry is like you walking out of one of Ray's crews that slang on the street and going to work for a rival crew ... Not going to happen with Ray. Once you're in, you're in, just like the mob."

"Well, Antoinette, it appears that you were able to just walk away."

"Yeah, but it came at a hell of a price, too. Besides, Ray has a long memory; it ain't over between us in his mind, I'm sure."

"So a war, just like that—over me?"

"Not *just* over you, Quincy. Don't look so surprised. I still would have to pull many strings and prod Victor on my end, but it could've worked. It's not like that's not what you want."

"No, Antoinette, it's not what I want. You think I want to be in the middle of this feud between you, your husband and Raymond James? I don't think so!"

"Well, the back up plan is what we need to talk about. If Raymond doesn't bite, the bottom line is, I want Victor out of the picture. Period!"

"You want me to kill Victor, so that we—you and I—can run Cut Throat Records, and I'm supposed to just believe that you're going to cut me in as an equal partner? Do I have it right, Toni?"

She reached up and grabbed a lock of her hair that dangled over her right eye, and twisted it tightly. "Yup," she replied, "you got it right, give or take, not that you have much of a choice, Quincy."

"And why in the hell should I trust yo' ass?"

K. Roland Williams

"For one thing, nigga, I got your cum leaking out of me as we speak. All I have to do is call the cops and say you raped me. I'm sure I even have a few bruises on my back where you slammed me into the shower wall earlier; you know how I like it rough, baby."

"Nobody will believe that shit, bitch!"

"Nigga, I got money from here to China. I can make people believe anything I want! Oh, and two ... remember the bloody clothes that I took from you? Well, let us just say I put them in a very safe place. That blood will implicate you in that murder. I'm sure if nothing else, it will make things really ugly for you. Now, Quincy, the cops never have to find out any of this shit, just do what I say and everything will be okay. To put it in perspective, nigga, I've got you in my pocket."

Quincy closed his eyes tight. He clenched his fists and unclenched them, feeling his heart rate increase and his body tense up like a steel coil ready to explode. With a huge exhalation, he replied, "Well, it seems you got me right where you want me. What do I need to do?"

Δ Δ Δ Δ

Kane and his pack of thugs were most definitely on the prowl. They had broken up into three vehicles, all making the rounds through the dark streets between The Melody Room and Xavier's house. Making sure to hit all of the alleys, side streets, cheap motels and hole-in-the-

K. Roland Williams

wall greasy spoons, they kept up the search. One of Kane's boys even sat stationed outside of Q's apartment building just in case he showed up there.

Kane reached out for the blunt and sucked in the dark smoke deeply until he choked and felt burning in the back of his throat. The Purple Haze was a fuckin' beast and most definitely his best seller right now. *No wonder the fiends buy his shit, it's the fuckin' bomb*, he thought.

"Keep your eyes open, Trey," he told the young hopper driving his truck.

"We're running out of time and we can't let the stopwatch quit ticking without coming back with the prize ... all of our asses depend on it."

The mobile phone vibrated hard on Kane's hip. He retrieved it from its cradle and saw Ray's cell phone number pop up on the caller ID. "Can't answer this call until I've got something better to tell him," Kane said. He ended the call with a mash of the disconnect button and dialed Renaldy's cell.

"Renaldy," the detective answered.

"Yeah, cop, anything yet?" Kane asked.

"Not yet, my boys are still looking though."

"Well, you might want to tell them to pick up the pace. I just spoke to my uncle, and he's about out of patience. In a minute, I think he's going to have us looking for your white ass. Don't forget the hole we dug."

"Look, we're doing all we can. We have the word out on the street through our informants. If anyone sees him,

K. Roland Williams

my phone will ring. So do me a fuckin' favor, and stop calling me. You stay on your side of the bridge and I'll stay on mine. If we hear anything I'll call *you*."

Δ Δ Δ Δ

"One, this is three, do you copy?" Renaldy's radio crackled to life through a hiss of static and broken words.

"Yes, I copy, go ahead, three."

"We've got something here. I called and checked in with LoJack again, and her car came up outside of the Four Seasons Hotel. I believe we got her ass now."

Renaldy sat up with excitement. "One to three, all right! Good fucking police work. I want you to take a position in front of the hotel, and I'll have the rest of the team there in under half an hour, so just sit tight. Oh yeah, the two grand bonus is yours." Renaldy figured that Quincy had dumped Kane's truck and had Antoinette Sweet pick him up there. She was hiding them at the Four Seasons, trying to lay low. *They aren't laying low enough though*, Renaldy thought to himself. *Thanks, LoJack, technology's a bitch, ain't it?*

"Two, four and five, this is one, we have our target. Everyone converge on the Four Seasons hotel in Georgetown. When on site, hold for further orders. I am en route, one out."

twenty

Quincy and Antoinette sat across from each other silently.

"You know you need help, right, Antoinette?"

"Help? Help! The only help I need right now is green and comes in the form of big-face hundred dollar bills! You know we can both come out ahead in this thing if you take a few minutes and stop being selfish, and really, I mean *really*, think this thing through."

Quincy ran all types of scenarios through his mind. They all came back rejected. Each one ended with him either going to jail or being zipped up in a body bag.

Quincy's thoughts were interrupted by a pounding at the door.

"Who in the fuck? No one knows we're here." Antoinette was startled but walked to the door, clearly nervous as hell about who might be banging on it like the police this early in the morning.

"Who is it?" Antoinette asked quietly as if she had

K. Roland Williams

been awakened by the banging. The voice on the other side was Philippe, the hotel manager. He sounded out of breath and frantic.

"Mrs. Sweet, it's me, Philippe. You have to open the door right now ... you don't have a lot of time," the man said in a thick Spanish accent. Antoinette opened the door and a short, mousy man in a neat jacket and slacks outfit stood there, his straight black hair swooped neatly to one side.

"Philippe, what's going on? What do you mean I don't have a lot of time? Time for what?"

"There are several men outside on their way in the hotel. My lot attendant saw them around your car a few minutes ago, and they're planning on coming in here. He heard your name mentioned as well. I didn't know what to do, so I had to come and tell you. You have been good to me for the years you have been staying here."

"Thanks for letting me know, I've got to go." Antoinette closed the door and yelled for Q to get his things together.

"We've got to go? We just got here," Q said as he gathered the gun, cell phone and wire. He placed them all in a white pillow case and slung the satchel over his right shoulder.

Δ Δ Δ Δ

The cops prepared to go into the hotel. As they stood

K. Roland Williams

there quickly going over their plan, one of the cops noticed a Lexus sitting in the hotel parking lot and the driver of the luxury sedan watching their every move. It was suspicious enough for a car to be idling in the lot of the hotel at this hour. The cop silently ran the plate number through the police database. The engine of the car quietly purred and the man inside watched the scene.

The driver knew he had to move quickly before they did; he didn't have a lot of time.

Δ Δ Δ Δ

As Antoinette opened the door, the imposing figure of a tall man appeared in the shadow of the doorway. It was Ricky Wright. He had followed Antoinette to the hotel—as it was his job to do—and it had taken him a while to finally figure out what room she was in. But now that he had her where he wanted her, the script was about to be flipped.

Ricky smiled an ominous smile at the uncomfortable-looking duo standing in the door of the room. Both Q and Antoinette looked startled and afraid of Ricky. At least that's what he convinced himself.

"What the fuck are you doing here, Ricky, following me again, you no-life-having punk?"

"Call me what you want, but you can save that shit for your husband. He's gonna want to ask you a few questions himself." Ricky's eyes were a darker shade of

K. Roland Williams

red than usual. Antoinette saw the devil each time she peered into the man's wide, crimson glare.

"Look, Ricky." Antoinette tried reasoning with the man. "We have to go, and go right now!"

Quincy grabbed Antoinette's wrist and tried to push past Ricky, who still stood stoic and intimidating in the doorway.

"Whoa, tough guy," Ricky said, producing a chrome .40 cal from beside his large Rocawear belt buckle. "We *are* leaving. What you think I'm here for? I'm here to save yaw asses. I know all about the cops downstairs mobilizing to come up here to grab your ass, Quincy. My police radio told me everything I needed to know. I got more channels on this bitch than Comcast. And I been watchin' from a distance. Let's bounce." Ricky waved his gun and motioned for Q and Antoinette to pass him.

"Where are we going?" Toni asked.

"We're gonna go to a safe place, a place where nobody will come and screw with you. Home, Antoinette. Cut Throat's office."

The three moved cautiously toward the rear emergency staircase.

"These cops will more than likely think to cover all the steps, but we don't really have much of a choice—we gotta get down to my car."

"Why are we riding with you, Ricky?" Antoinette asked.

"Because the cops are probably all over your car in

the parking lot, Toni." Quincy answered.

"Stop all the chatter. They're going to hear us a mile away." Ricky carefully pushed open the door to the rear steps and looked down the narrow stairway that led to the first floor. "Okay, it looks like it's clear for the moment. Hopefully they think they're catching you off-guard so they won't be that thorough." Ricky led them down each level, his gun ready to blaze in the event a cop rounded the corner. Fourteen floors to the bottom.

Quincy eased his own gun out of the satchel as they descended the stairs. Slipping it in his belt under the shirt that was given to him, he felt more secure, though he knew the weapon couldn't have too many more bullets left in it after the gun fight with Kane's crew in the alley.

The three finally reached the bottom of the steps with still no sign of anyone, cops or otherwise.

"All right, we need to go across the lobby and find the door to the rear of the hotel. That's where I'm parked, and it's the only way out."

"Ricky, I think I'm gonna go my own fuckin' way."

Ricky turned around to find Quincy standing there with his own nine millimeter pointed dead center of his chest. "Where'd you get that thing?" Ricky asked. "Don't be an idiot, you need me right now. I'm your only way out of here," Ricky tried to reason with Quincy. "What are you going to do, run away on foot? And go where exactly? You have nowhere to fuckin' go, nigga!"

K. Roland Williams

"I think he's actually right, Q," Antoinette said.

"Yeah, Q, put the gun down." Ricky raised his own gun up slowly to match Quincy's move. "Tick, tock, tick, tock, Quincy, the cops remember?"

Quincy breathed hard and lowered the weapon, sliding it down into his waistband again.

"A'ight, you convinced me. Let's roll out, fuck it."

Δ Δ Δ Δ

Renaldy and his crew of crooked cops all poured out of the elevator on the fourteenth floor casually, expecting very little opposition. They even had a key to the room, supplied by the front-desk clerk after he was paid with three crisp twenty-dollar bills.

"Here is the room right here," Baptiste whispered.

The door to the room was cracked open, and no sound came from within. All the cops took defensive postures, weapons ready, and gestured with their hands who would enter first and how. Typically, a kicked-in door and a flash bang grenade would be in order for a surprise take down, but since they were not supposed to even be there and they were not SWAT, they would do it the old-fashioned way.

The five officers entered the room quietly but quickly, all taking a different room in the massive suite. Very little was left that even gave the impression that anyone had been there at all. The bed was a mess and dirty towels were strewn across the floor, but no Quincy and no Antoinette Sweet.

"Toss the room and look for a wire and receiver. You two go downstairs and cover the front and rear. They can't be too far. Keep an eye on Mrs. Sweet's car. We'll take the stairs down. We *cannot* lose them—we're too fucking close!" Renaldy panted hard, his breathing labored. He was clearly nervous about possibly losing Quincy. After all, his life was on the line.

"I need a fucking cigarette," he said as he lit up. "All right, Mr. Underwood, where have you crawled away to this time?"

Δ Δ Δ Δ

"Get in, you two." Ricky unlocked the door to his Lexus and looked around to make sure that the coast was clear. No cops were anywhere to be seen. The shit seemed too fucking easy.

Antoinette and Quincy got into his car and Ricky pulled away without incident. He picked up the phone and dialed a number. "Yeah, it's me, I got her this time, and she was with Quincy like you knew she would be. We're en route."

Quincy knew he did not want to be taken to Victor Sweet now. *Fuck, what else can happen tonight?* he thought to himself. Before Quincy could pull the nine millimeter from his belt to stop Ricky from driving to

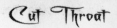

wherever Victor was, Ricky had pulled his own Smith & Wesson. Ricky's gun was pointed directly at Quincy stomach, and he was quite sure that Ricky would shoot him dead on the spot without hesitation; he had that coldness looming behind those blood-red eyes of his, that give-me-a-fuckin'-reason look that street niggaz, killers, had.

"Give me your gun, Quincy, and don't move too fast. I don't just follow this bitch around for a living, I do other things, too, like take care of punk-ass niggaz like you. Please don't test me, dunn."

Quincy complied and handed the gun over to Ricky without hesitation.

Antoinette sucked her teeth from the back seat of the Lex. "Quincy, you didn't even try and argue with him or nothing, huh? Just gonna give up the gun, huh?"

"Shut up, it didn't have any bullets in it anyway," Quincy said.

"Well, damn, he didn't have to know that." Antoinette turned her head and rolled her eyes.

Quincy held on tight to his pillowcase and looked out the window of the Lexus. "I'm tired of fuckin' running now, Antoinette. Time to get to the end of this fuckin' game, and whatever happens, so be it."

twenty-one

Victor was sitting with his back to the door in one of the three Cut Throat Records state-of-the-art recording studios. He was wrapping up a phone call on his mobile and listening to one of his artists over his Bose sound system when Ricky, Quincy and Antoinette walked fearfully into the door. The technician sitting at the soundboard spun around, his headphones cocked sideways. He nodded to the group then went back to work. Their all-night mix-down sessions were nothing new; Victor was a workaholic and everyone knew it.

"Victor, we made it in," Ricky said. Before he could say another word, Victor raised his right index finger to stop him from speaking. Ricky still held Quincy at gunpoint, the gun a few feet from Quincy's back. The gun was more for show than anything because Quincy wasn't resisting anyway. "We were ducking cops and shit, it was crazy."

"One minute, I said, nigga! Listen to this riff right

K. Roland Williams

here." Victor held his eyes closed tightly and felt every note of the music.

The song played for a few bars and Desiree took it to the bridge with a high soprano note that descended several octaves down into the alto range. Victor bobbed his head to the beat of the melodic, mid tempo track, his back still to the group that stood in his multi-million-dollar studio.

Eventually, Victor turned around, his eyes now trained on the nervous expression on his wife's face. Victor's twenty carat diamond necklace shimmered in the studio lights as he moved toward the small group like a panther stalking a group of gazelle. Vic looked at his wife as if he weren't surprised to find out that she had been cheating on him and shook his head with a disappointed, yet amused look on his face.

"Victor, give me a minute to explain. It's not the way it looks."

"What, let me guess, you left our home in the middle of the night to meet a nigga at a hotel room, and it's not what *I* think. Ricky, get this bitch out of here. Oh yeah, and make a few calls to get some of the fellas down here just in case those cops looking for his ass show up here trippin'." Victor Sweet motioned for Ricky to remove his wife and take her into another room.

Antoinette could not believe her ears. Her own husband had called her a bitch. Victor and Antoinette had had countless arguments over the years they'd been together, but he had never called her by that name. He had also never caught her fucking around on him before—it had always been the other way around.

"Oh, hell no, nigga, have you lost your mind?" Antoinette was stunned.

She was yelling as Ricky pulled her into the next room, kicking and screaming to be let go and put down. Her voice faded with the closing of the soundproof door of the studio.

"Yo, Chris ... Chris!" Victor tried to get the attention of his sound technician whose back was turned as he mixed the track, but apparently, the music was too loud in his headphones for him to hear anything. Victor kicked his chair to get his undivided attention.

"Get out of here. Matter of fact, take the rest of the morning off."

The man knew not to question his celebrity boss. He walked quickly around Quincy and exited the room, earphones still attached to his head, cord dangling.

Quincy stood there, seemingly fearless, unaffected by Victor's obvious anger. Victor stood staring at Quincy, debating on what to do to him.

"Before you do anything crazy, you might want to get all of the facts together."

"Nigga, let's see if I have it all right. You are fucking my wife, and you got the balls to come in here and talk to me about what I should do for you. I'll tell you what I *should* do, nigga." Victor walked to the wall and pushed

K. Roland Williams

a button. A panel slid away, revealing a safe. Victor rotated the dial, released the door and removed a nickel-plated .45. Dropping it to his side, he continued talking to Quincy. "I should cut your ass up in little pieces and feed you to the piranhas in that tank over there."

"True enough, your wife did approach me and I didn't walk away from her, but what's more important is what I have to give you." Quincy reached slowly into the pillowcase that he still had clutched in his hand and pulled the small black box out, placing it down in front of Victor on the table. Victor raised his gun, carefully holding it on Quincy while he fiddled through his sack.

"What's this shit, nigga?" Victor looked into Q's eyes and debated calling Ricky into the room to take care of Quincy. Instead, Victor allowed his curiosity to give the man a pass, if only temporarily.

"You have about five seconds to tell me what the fuck you're talking about before I cut the lights off on your ass." Victor sat back down in his chair, placing the gun on the mixing board as the female vocalist started another track. This one was a slow cut that Victor wrote himself. He pressed the pause button on the high-tech computer, silencing the music to give Quincy the floor.

Quincy pressed the play button on the digital recorder and allowed it to go from beginning to end.

Quite a while later, Victor sat with his hands pressed together in a temple position. The most important recordings in the studio now were the ones that Quincy

K. Roland Williams

had on the small device. A wide variety of voices, most of which Victor recognized, were discussing things, ranging from drugs and extortion all the way to several cold-blooded murders.

One person stood out amongst the rest on the tape—Victor's wife, Antoinette. Quincy had set the tape up to record Antoinette at the hotel room, thinking that she might say something worth getting on tape.

She discussed the finer details of how she wanted Victor dead and how Quincy was going to do it, or risk going to jail for the rest of his own life. She spoke with malicious intent toward her husband. Her voice was as cold if not colder than the recordings of Raymond James speaking of murder. Victor couldn't believe his own ears.

Once the tape stopped and the digital voices faded in the sound-proofed walls of the studio, Victor was the first to speak. "So what do you think letting me hear this is going to do for you? Do you think it will make me forget about the fact that you fucked my wife?"

"I'm not trying to make you forget anything. What I *am* trying to do is give you information about a woman who wants you out of the picture. Not to mention give you information about Raymond James and how badly he wants you dead!"

"Raymond, fuck Raymond. I should have finished his ass ten years ago!" Victor exclaimed with the same anger that he had back when the actual event took place. "Had I cut his throat another inch deeper, he

K. Roland Williams

wouldn't even be here now. Do I look like someone who is that easily shaken by some other nigga? How far do you think I would have gotten in my business by being concerned with what other people might do to me?"

"It was you who cut Ray's throat? Oh shit!" Quincy was stunned at the information, but it all made perfect sense now. The feud between Victor and Raymond and Raymond's past relationship with Antoinette were the reasons for the war in the first place. It hadn't been power, drugs or money, but the love of one woman.

"Well, don't act like if the shoe was on the other foot you wouldn't do the same fuckin' thing. As many women as you fuck, Victor ... don't act like you don't understand opportunity," Quincy said, feeling brave. "You're as much an opportunist as I am."

"Yeah, true enough. I do understand opportunity. How do you think I got where I am today? Seizing opportunity is a gift *and* a talent, but that don't give you a pass for fuckin' my wife! I've killed folks for a hell of a lot less!"

"Victor, I ain't going to beg you for shit. I been through some crazy-ass shit the last few days, and I don't really give a fuck right now. All I want is what I always wanted ... to sing, that's it." Quincy didn't hesitate, and he didn't show an ounce of fear. He spoke from the heart, and Victor felt that he was being sincere about his situation.

"I'm bringing this information to you because I know

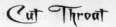

you can use it—to look out for yourself and to possibly help me out of this bullshit situation that I've gotten myself into."

A few minutes went by. They were the longest minutes that Quincy had ever experienced.

"Rewind the tape to the part where Antoinette tried to talk you into killing me or she would tell the cops you raped her." Victor seemed to be slightly amused, and he redirected his attention to the FBI wire and away from Quincy.

Quincy exhaled deeply and complied with Victor Sweet's request. It appeared that he might have finally gotten a break in all of this shit. He didn't want to get comfortable yet, but he did feel his heart beating again, the blood rushing through his veins and the numbness in his skull starting to subside. He might get out of this shit after all.

K. Roland Williams

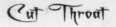

twenty-two

Raymond James paced the living room of his palatial estate like a lion in a cage and waited for the latest information on the search for Quincy and the evidence that Quincy had in his possession. That kind of evidence could possibly put Raymond, Kane and his crew in federal prison for the rest of their lives. He made several calls to both Renaldy and Kane, but no one was answering the phone, nor were they returning his calls. His patience was running thinner by the moment and his anger was starting to boil over. Fear had never been a word that Ray recognized. In fact, *I ain't scared of shit unless you fear it for me,* had been the man's motto his entire life.

Now, with the murder of a federal undercover agent at his night club, the sloppy on-the-spot killing of a club employee as a cover-up and Quincy running around with evidence of God knew what other crimes Raymond had committed, who knew what the future would hold?

No money in the world would save him if the Feds found out the *truth* about the slaying of one of their own.

Loose ends had to be tied up, and tied up quickly. Raymond sipped on his rum and considered his options. It was simple, really. Anyone who knew anything about these crimes would have to go. That held true for Renaldy, Quincy, Antoinette and her husband, Victor.

Raymond allowed his mind to slip back to the days when Antoinette had belonged to him. Life was good in the early days when he and Victor Sweet had built their drug empire from the ground up. They had been two young, hungry, grimy niggaz from the projects when they started with only a few ounces of coke that had been given to them on consignment. They flipped it until they had taken their own corners and the respect of the local hustlers, players and killers of the D.C. streets. After a short period of time, they earned enough to get their own connect with the Columbian drug cartel and started moving major weight.

Raymond and Victor had been the original gangsters, stackin' their paper and killing any nigga who made the mistake of getting in their way. Nevertheless, the ol' saying was true—"with more money comes more problems"—and Victor had allowed a piece of ass to come between him and Raymond. That piece of ass was Antoinette.

Bitches had come and gone for both men, but Antoinette had been different; she held Ray down from

K. Roland Williams

the very beginning when they didn't have a thin dime between them, back when Raymond was the brains behind the operation and Victor was the muscle. Raymond never knew what a woman as beautiful as Antoinette saw in him, but back then, it felt real enough. But Raymond knew that enough money could make anything feel real, especially when a slick-ass, ambitious woman from the ghetto, who had never had a thing in her life, got greedy.

Raymond never even saw the set up coming. Victor had gotten to Antoinette at some point, and she went willingly with the much more handsome and charismatic man. When Raymond found out that his partner was fucking his woman, it was too late; in a final altercation between the two men, Victor overpowered Raymond and cut his throat with a twelve-inch butcher knife, leaving him in a pool of his own blood to die. Pussy was power, not money like everyone thought. Raymond had to learn that the hard way, and it had almost cost him his life.

Victor and Raymond had been business partners and, he thought, niggaz for life—blood in, blood out. However, that whore, Antoinette, had been trouble from day one, with her overly abundant smiles and excessively friendly conversations with Victor when she thought Ray wasn't around. It seemed the pretty boy always got the girl, and Raymond knew that he had not been the pretty boy. He ran his finger over the scar on his throat and thought about the night when he and Victor had that final confrontation.

Soon after Victor cut Raymond's throat with that knife, Antoinette and Victor had married and she took the last name Sweet. They honeymooned in Hawaii while Raymond lay scarcely alive in intensive care, barely holding on to his life.

Five years was a long time to suffer the loss of a woman, a business and an ego. It was time to get even with Victor and Antoinette. There was nothing that would stop Raymond. He had bided his time long enough—he never forgot and he never forgave. He was not prepared to take another loss at this point in his life. Too many sacrifices had been made for him to give up now.

Raymond's home phone finally rang and he answered, knowing that it was Kane. Raymond wasted no time getting to the point. "Well, do you have Quincy and do you have the tape recorder? There is only one answer that I want to fuckin' hear."

It was clear to Raymond after several seconds of hesitation on the part of his nephew, that Kane had failed him. He said, "You have a few hours before the FBI opens their office doors downtown, and I wouldn't be surprised if Quincy is standing there in the lobby waiting for someone to talk to."

Kane rubbed his shoulder and remembered Neecy's bullet passing through his flesh there. It still burned as if

K. Roland Williams

the gunpowder and lead had just been fired into his body. The sling that Ray's unofficial doctor had given him was irritating, and he felt the need to take it off, but the thought of the wound opening up and pouring out more blood made him keep it in place.

"We're close to getting him. We just missed him at the Four Seasons on Pennsylvania and Twenty-Eighth. I got Renaldy and a bunch of his cops on the case. Renaldy just called and updated me. I think that bitch, Antoinette, is with him again because Renaldy has her Benz down there at the hotel. He seems to think that they were just picked up a few minutes ago."

"How do you know it's Antoinette's car?"

"It has *Cut Throat* on the plates, it's her."

Irritated by the words on her car plates, Ray went off the deep end. "You fucked up again. I'm starting to think I don't even need you around anymore, what fuckin' good are you?" Raymond yelled into the receiver, trying to kill his nephew with his words. "You're fuckin' useless to me! Why don't you run a fuckin' ad in the newspaper? No, better yet, put Quincy's face on a milk carton: *Have you seen this night club singer? He has evidence that might put everyone in fuckin' jail!* You got other people involved in this chase?"

"Useless, Ray? I don't think so. Renaldy got them involved, that was *his* call, Ray, not mine," Kane said, lying to Ray. "Who in the fuck has been doing all your dirt in the streets all these years? Taking care of the competition, making the re-ups, setting up the crack houses, making the collections, burying the bodies? *Me*, that's who! All you do now is sit back and wait for me to bring you the money! You know what, Ray? You never gave me the credit that I deserve. You been rich so long, you've fuckin' forgotten what the grind is like out here in the streets."

"Nigga, I made dem streets ... shit, I am dem fuckin' streets! Every crack you see in the pavement is from my boots, nigga, from the work I put in on those streets, way before you was even thought of! Way before my sister ever pushed your sorry, useless, bastard ass out of her pussy! She wasn't shit, and you ain't gonna never be shit! Nothing more than I allow your ass to be."

Raymond's words made Kane instinctively reach for his gun, even though his uncle was miles away in the relative safety of his home. Kane had never heard his uncle speak so venomously about him, and never about his own sister. That was a no-no to Kane. No one spoke that way about his now-deceased mother and lived to tell the tale.

"Ray, I know you are stressed right now, so I'm gonna overlook what you just said—"

"Overlook what, nigga? I will say it again for the cheap seats! *I* am the fuckin' boss around here! *I* put this shit together, not you! You work for *me*, not the other fuckin' way around!"

"I'm sorry you feel that way, Ray," Kane said in a

K. Roland Williams

muted tone. He fumed and allowed his uncle's words to marinate for a while. As a last ditch effort to appease his uncle, Kane interjected, "Ray, one of Renaldy's boys saw a suspicious car parked the last time we knew where Antoinette and Quincy were. The plate came back connected to Victor Sweet. It was Victor's boy Ricky Wright's car. They're probably with him now, maybe at Victor's office. There's no evidence they went anywhere else."

"Why you just tellin' me shit? I want you here in thirty minutes. Get your crew en route and make sure that they are strapped with everything in the arsenal. We need to make a run."

Δ Δ Δ Δ

Kane called his extensive team of hoods and slingers and assembled them in front of his uncle's home for a final effort to find Quincy. They were twenty strong and stood around smoking and talking quietly amongst themselves, all growing a bit impatient with the wait and the last minute change of their routine. More importantly, they all knew that they were losing money, lots of money.

The task was important enough to shut down the many southeastern D.C. drug corners and crack houses that the crews worked all night and leave them bare and drug free for a few hours. Kane operated those corners and knew the risk associated with leaving them unattended, even for a second. It wouldn't take a rival crew long to move in on the already well-established corners with their own product if anyone knew they had just walked away from them. They would change the color of the caps, and Kane's Black Fever would be replaced with the Yellow Yo that the Dominicans were pushing hard on their established blocks.

Now was not the time to show even an ounce of weakness. The streets were watchin'.

Raymond still fuckin' up the money, Kane thought to himself as he waited with his boys for Raymond to come out of his house. *He should have never trusted that crooked-ass cop, and he never should've been running his fuckin' mouth at the club in the first fuckin' place, getting recorded.*

While Kane waited, he dialed Renaldy to check on his progress. They still had a chance to silence Quincy and Antoinette Sweet, but they were all running out of time. The sun would be up in three hours and Monday morning was rapidly approaching.

Raymond stepped out of his door in all black—jeans, Timberlands and a casual shirt—with a Benelli M1 shotgun in hand and a nine in the small of his back. The scowl on his face showed that he clearly meant business.

He approached the long row of SUVs, luxury cars and hoopties that sat in a semi-circle around the marble fountain in his front yard. Most of the lower-level hus-

K. Roland Williams

tlers and lookouts who worked for Kane had never been this close to this kind of money and had never even met Raymond before. He was still a legend to most of the young men, and they couldn't believe their eyes when he came up to them with street gear on, ready to go to war. A man at his level would never get his hands dirty under any circumstances. Most of these youngins would have gladly given their lives for Raymond. Kane was the first to speak.

"We're all here and ready to go, but I wanted to talk to you about letting a few of these cats go back to the corners to hold them down until we can get back out there. You know what could happen if we stay gone too long."

Clearly irritated, Raymond looked at his nephew and exhaled deeply like he had just completed a long run. "Just let me do the thinking, Kane; I'll take care of it from now on." There was a vacancy that resided there behind Raymond's eyes that Kane had never seen before. They were void of life. It was almost like looking into the eyes of a dead man.

Raymond stood over the men like a general commanding his troops. Kane noticed that Ray still had that alpha male presence. He still had that same street instinct Kane remembered so well.

The men rallied quickly and went over their objectives, then got into their vehicles to go to war.

"Well, good having you back, Ray," one of his

crewmembers said. "I haven't seen you with a shotgun in your hand since that problem with the Jamaican crew who tried to move into our territory last year."

"Yeah, well, get used to it. I'm back." Raymond got behind the driver's seat of his Range Rover and told Kane to ride with him. Kane did so hesitantly, carefully watching the shotty that sat loaded on Ray's lap.

"I guess they think they safe at Victor's studio?" Kane asked.

"Well, guess what, they're far from safe. Victor has gotten lax and sloppy since he traded slangin' dope for slangin' music. His security will be weak, and we should be able to walk right in there with very little problem."

Kane looked into the truck's side mirror and saw a caravan of bouncing headlights trailing Ray's black truck. Raymond's boys were rolling mob deep and would stand out like a fuckin' sore thumb driving through the streets like a trail of ants going to a picnic. Kane was more worried than ever. He made sure to keep his eyes open for the police, his uncle, and more importantly, the menacing black street sweeper that sat comfortably in Ray's lap.

Raymond ordered Kane to call Renaldy and pass the information that they were all to meet up at the studio of Cut Throat Records. Renaldy and his people were already there waiting for Kane and his crew. Kane now had to be concerned about walking into Victor's spot blind and naked. Renaldy had reported a few cars going

K. Roland Williams

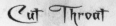
into the parking lot of Cut Throat Records and armed men being at the door. Ray didn't seem to care much for the details, and fuck the fact that Victor and his people would be there and might not want Quincy to be taken.

The caravan proceeded through the rapidly-waking city like a funeral procession toward Cut Throat Records. Kane watched apprehensively as his uncle potentially drove them all into early graves.

twenty-three

The sun was just starting to peek slowly above the horizon as the first hint of dawn revealed its bouquet of muted colors. Two armed men stood in the doorway of the studio and put on their game faces the second the first of the police cars pulled up in the lot. The police noticed that the Lexus from the Four Seasons parking lot was there, as was Victor's Bentley coupe. One of the guards at the door to the label was on his cell phone immediately, more than likely giving a report of the number of cars and men that were about to enter the gate.

Raymond cut his eyes sharply the second he saw the logo on the sign outside of the studio. The picture of a knife against a man's throat on the large sign made Ray reach for his own neck, a grim reminder of Victor's obvious disrespect for Ray, using their personal battle as a joke. It fueled the fire raging inside of Raymond, making him angrier by the second. He reached for the shotgun

K. Roland Williams

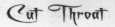

on his lap as he turned the truck off and prepared to get out into the humid early morning air and finally get closure on the one thing that had haunted him for so long.

Thunder buckled the heavens from a distance as storm clouds rolled in from the east. The air was dense and made it hard to breathe. Mother Nature even seemed to be making an appearance for the final showdown.

"How do you want to do this?" Kane asked before they exited the truck.

"You know what, he already knows we're here, so let's just go right through the front door," Raymond replied.

"Tell these other niggaz to sit tight, hold down the fort out here. Me, you and Renaldy can go in to get this all straightened out. If they act stupid about handing over the tape, make sure that yo' boys are ready to come in here blasting if they get the call."

Kane called his lieutenants and passed along Ray's message to sit tight. He tried to get the attention of Renaldy, who was sitting in his car on a mobile. The other cops with Renaldy were told to sit tight also and remain in the lot with Kane's dope boys, a thought that didn't sit very well with them.

Surprisingly, Ray, Kane and Renaldy had no trouble getting into the front door. Victor's two massive armed men allowed them entry only after patting them down and insisting that they leave their weapons outside in

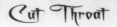
the parking lot.

Renaldy was the only one able to keep his gun. His cop status allowed him that privilege.

Victor passed along the message that he would be unarmed as well, but they would have to just trust that. The larger of the two guards spoke into a small throat mic and informed Ricky of the situation. He met them at the door and escorted them to Victor himself.

Ricky and Kane, both underbosses in their separate organizations, gritted on each other from the second that they saw one another. They recognized each other from the street. It was a very small town when it came down to it all, particularly in their line of work. You had to know who the players were in the business, even if it was from a distance. They had a mutual respect for each other, a street respect, but sized each other up anyway.

Ricky escorted the three men to the record label's conference room to wait for Victor. Raymond continued to seethe. He started to regret his decision to come to the studio this way, rushing into this confrontation out of anger and desperation. But fuck it, he was there now and would deal with it as he dealt with most things. He wished he had the shotgun now to blow Victor's fucking head off as he walked through the door. He could kill Victor finally, and then go and have a good breakfast and get on with his life—a quick murder, eggs, toast and orange juice. Ray figured it would be the perfect start to his day. No more videos, no more awards shows for

K. Roland Williams

Victor, nothing, just a cold, long sleep for his backstabbing, throat-slashing ass!

But he also knew that the priority now was Quincy and the evidence that he had in his possession. That's what Ray wanted desperately, and he was almost willing to trade his black soul to get that evidence. He laughed at the thought of doing business with Satan himself because he had bargained with his soul in the past, and he would never be able to trade what the devil already owned. It wasn't just about revenge now, it was about survival, too.

The gold and platinum plaques on the walls were a testament to Victor's success in the music industry, and the boardroom of the label would rival that of any major Fortune 500 company. Raymond stood and waited for Victor and Quincy to enter the room. The sound of throats clearing nervously and shuffling feet could be heard. Ricky stood guard, arms crossed, hoping that Antoinette behaved herself and remained in the back room where she was told to stay.

Victor eventually walked through the door with Quincy in tow. Ray's eyes were daggers dipped in lava. He was the first to break the uncomfortable silence in the room.

"I won't waste time fucking around here. Quincy, you have something that belongs to me, and I want it right now. I will not ask twice." Raymond waited for Quincy to respond. His hope was that Quincy would simply turn

K. Roland Williams

over the wire. He wasn't confident that he would, but Ray figured he would ask and pray that Vic would stay out of this part of their issue with each other. Then he would concern himself with all the other loose ends and satisfy his hunger for vengeance.

"Raymond, you might want to watch your tone—you in my house. As for Quincy, he is on my team now and anything you have to say to him you can say to me." Victor challenged Ray and prodded him to respond.

"Nigga, I'm not talking to you! Don't worry, I'll get to yo' ass soon enough!" Raymond pounded his fists into the glass table, still staring into Q's eyes, trying to provoke a reaction. He stood there dressed in all black, his huge arms down with his fists on the table.

Quincy remained silent. He seemed to be enjoying the frustration in Ray's eyes and the anger that his having the wire and the upper hand brought.

"Raymond, you don't quite understand the situation that you're in right now. Things are not what they appear to be," Victor said.

Kane began to get impatient and Renaldy stayed silent as if he were scared to open his mouth. He had reached the point of no return and had fallen as low as a cop could. He was just holding on for dear life at this point.

"All I know is I have twenty armed killers outside just waiting for the signal to make their move, and if I don't get what I came here for, they will be in here faster than

K. Roland Williams

I can point my finger at you." Raymond grew tired of the wait. "Fuck this shit. Renaldy, get the fuckin' wire from Quincy. It's time you earn your fuckin' keep." Ray decided to play his hand and use his trump card, knowing that the cop had his heat on him.

Renaldy hesitated, acting as if he weren't sure of what his next move should be. Kane watched and waited for him to follow Ray's orders, but the cop just stood there looking at Victor.

"Renaldy!" Kane yelled. "You heard what my uncle said. Go over there and do some cop shit, you got your gun."

Renaldy swallowed hard then moved toward the far side of the conference table and around to where Quincy, Victor and Ricky now stood. Reaching Quincy, he turned around to face Kane and Raymond. His face was calm and he made no effort to touch Quincy in any way. He quietly looked at Victor and then back to Raymond.

"Like I said, Ray, you don't quite know the gravity of the situation here." Victor had a grin on his perfectly chiseled face, his perfect celebrity smile growing wider by the second as if he could not contain himself.

"What the fuck is going on, cop? Have you forgotten I know where your daughter goes to college? I think I'll make a trip up there to visit her personally." Ray's threat fell on deaf ears. Though Renaldy showed little concern, his heart pumped hard enough to explode in his chest.

K. Roland Williams

"You know your problem, Ray?" Renaldy said. "You don't know when you've lost the game. That's why I'm over here on this side of the table. Mr. Sweet was smart enough to listen to me when I called him a few hours ago and told him what your intentions were and that you were on your way here with all of us. Kane told me that you were planning to kill me, and probably my daughter, too, for all I know. I needed protection from you and he made me an offer that I ... just couldn't refuse, and here I am."

"You rotten, double-dealing, crooked-ass cop. You can't trust nobody these days." Ray looked at Kane. "Fuck this shit, let's get out of here, Kane," Ray said. "We *will* be back!"

"Oh and don't think about bringing those goons from outside in here," Renaldy said. "Let's see, right about now they should all be loading into the backs of a few paddy wagons that I arranged for right before we came inside."

Kane remembered Renaldy on the phone right before he got out of his car and walked into the building.

Victor smiled as he grabbed the remote control for the video surveillance camera in the front lot and turned on the sixty-inch plasma television that hung neatly on the wall. The clear screen came to life and showed a sea of flashing lights in front of Cut Throat Records. An entire squad of cops, four of which were Renaldy's part-ners who had remained behind to coordinate the mas-

K. Roland Williams

sive busts, was arresting all of Kane's men. The drug dealers had enough guns, drugs and paraphernalia to put them all in jail for a long time. Several of the men had warrants and were suspects in a variety of local crimes.

To Kane's surprise, they all went downtown without a single gunshot being fired. They were caught off-guard by the last minute set up that Renaldy arranged on his drive to Cut Throat. Victor turned the television off and smiled at Raymond.

"I told you, Ray, that you didn't know what was really going on. It would appear that I beat you again. You just don't get it, do you? You underestimated me then, and you still underestimate me. I always know when to make my move. You, on the other hand, are always slow on the trigger! Oh, and the tape that Quincy has, I'll personally make sure that the authorities get this little piece of evidence!" Victor crossed his muscular arms as if to say he had finally won, there was nothing else that needed to be done. Checkmate!

"Fuck that! You know what? I'm not going out like this!" Raymond ran his hand over his now-sweating bald head. His eyes shifted in his sockets and for the first time, he looked afraid. He started to make a move for the conference room door.

"Kane, we can still get out of here. I am not going to jail. Not after all that I have been through!" Raymond motioned for his young nephew to join him in his escape from the studio. He was clearly desperate because there was nowhere to run. The entire building was surrounded by cops, Renaldy had seen to that. And Ray wouldn't get far on foot. A 280 pound man running around the streets of D.C. would stand out. Before he reached the door, he stopped and turned, looking at the group that stood observing him.

"You dirty motherfuckers!" Raymond charged the group of men like a raging bull. He was able to knock Ricky to the ground, and with his full speed and weight, he punched Renaldy in the jaw so hard that he was thrown into a glass table that was up against the back wall, shattering it into a million pieces. Renaldy lay in the debris, unconscious from the blow.

Raymond and Victor collided and grappled like two juggernauts, both men equal in size and fuming with hatred for the other. Quincy reeled back from the attack and reached for the pillowcase that sat on one of the conference room chairs. Victor swung and missed Raymond's face by inches as Raymond hit Victor in the gut with a powerful punch that took the breath from the younger man. Victor dropped to his knee, trying to catch his breath.

Raymond was in another world. His anger was uncontrollable and had grown to that of an animal. All that was visible to him was the red hue of hatred. It clouded his vision and coursed heavily through his blood. Raymond's soul was ablaze with revenge. Victor

K. Roland Williams

tried to grab the side of the table to pull himself up, but before he could do it, Raymond was on top of him in seconds, pinning him to the ground with all of his weight.

Raymond grabbed a stainless steel letter opener that sat at the head of the table, apparently left there by the secretary. Raymond sat on Victor's chest, pinning his arms back, holding his throat tightly with his left hand, squeezing harder each second, trying to force the last of Victor's air from his lungs. He waved the six-inch sharpened blade with his right hand over Victor's eye. Victor tried to move, but Raymond's weight was too much for the man.

"Now who has a clear understanding of the situation, motherfucker?" Raymond was in a haze of fury and was seconds from driving the blade into Victor's throat, payback for the years of pain that Victor had caused Raymond, for his deceit and disloyalty.

"Game over, you bitch-ass nigga!" Raymond screamed as he drew back high with the letter opener. Victor prepared himself for the deathblow. He could not believe how he ended up on the floor so quickly. He cursed his own arrogance, but it didn't matter now. His last thoughts played through his mind in a light-speed blur, his adrenaline bursting through his veins and arteries. He realized right then, the moment before his death, that he had never felt so alive in his life. He was surprised to see a vision of Antoinette in his mind. The man had never been one for regrets, but his last thought was that he should have never called his wife a bitch, despite the fact that she had slept with Quincy, and the fact that she wanted him dead.

"Raymond, do it ... please, do it!" Antoinette said under her breath as she appeared in the doorway, watching the two men fight to the death. Ricky pulled his gun out and tried to get a bead on Raymond from across the expansive conference room, but Ray was moving and Antoinette had gotten between him and Raymond almost purposely to ruin his chance of blasting Ray.

She walked in right in time to see Raymond reverse the scene from all those years ago. This time it would be Raymond plunging steel into Victor. This would be her moment. Raymond would finally do it—he would finally kill Victor. Her strategy had worked after all, and she felt no remorse, nothing but joyous delight and plans for her bright, bright future as a single, rich woman.

Quincy ran forward to grab Ray's arm. Ricky was still trying to get a shot at Ray and shoved Antoinette out of his way. She fell hard into the corner of the large mahogany conference table, her head colliding with the heavy wood. A sickening thump resounded as she bounced off the table and landed unconscious on the floor, blood pouring from the gash in her skull.

Raymond plunged the knife toward Victor's throat, but his hand seemed to move in slow motion.

The sudden gunshot was explosive and startled everyone in the room. A burst of warm red blood

K. Roland Williams

splashed Victor's face. Raymond's hand stopped in mid thrust. His eyes took on a look of confusion. He looked around, reached to the back of his head with his hand to where the pain was, where the hole was now starting to leak brain matter, and he tried to speak, but no words were able to form, the part of his brain that controlled speech now destroyed by the bullet lodged there. His eyes retreated to the back of his skull, and he lurched forward and fell to one side of Victor, twitching and dead.

Victor sat up and inhaled gulps of air deeply and greedily, his face awash with Raymond's blood.

Kane stood there with Renaldy's gun in his hand, shaking. He still hadn't processed the fact that he had just killed his own flesh and blood. Kane had removed the gun from Renaldy's holster while the cop was knocked out and Victor and Raymond were tussling. He saw it as an opportunity to do what he knew had to be done. Raymond was not going to allow Kane to live through all of this. Ray would probably have given him up to the cops the second they were arrested once the cops made their way inside.

Kane ran the argument that he had with his uncle through his head. He looked down at his uncle's still-twitching body and spat. "Talking about my mother, nigga. I ain't shit, nigga? What! Look at you now! I'm here and you ain't!"

Victor wiped the blood from his eyes to make sure he

was seeing correctly. Victor had been saved by Raymond's right-hand man and couldn't believe it. He saw Antoinette's body at the end of the table with Ricky trying to wake her; she wasn't moving. Victor jumped up and ran to Toni, calling her name, but she didn't respond. He shook her and yelled for someone to call an ambulance.

Renaldy still lay unconscious on the conference room floor. The security guards rushed in with weapons drawn, demanding that Kane lower his gun.

Renaldy started to come to, slowly and groggily. He stood to find Raymond dead, Antoinette Sweet unconscious and Victor covered in blood.

"What the fuck happened? Was I knocked out for a week? Who let Kane have a gun?" Renaldy tried to shake off the confusion as if he had awoken to find himself still asleep but in a bad dream. "And who put a hole in Raymond's head?"

Victor kneeled next to Toni's limp body. She was breathing shallowly. Victor pressed a bunch of paper towels up against her wound. Kane looked baffled and nervous and tried to run every word through his mind that he had ever spoken in front of Quincy over the last two years.

The two FBI agents from Neecy's shooting investigation came through the door of the conference room, guns drawn. The Metro police were right behind them.

"How did you know when to come?" Quincy asked

K. Roland Williams

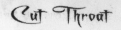
the FBI agents.

"When you turned on the wire, we started to track the GPS chip inside of it and the signal led us all around town, from where you dumped Renaldy's police car to the Four Seasons and eventually here. We also pulled the video surveillance tape from the bank across from the nightclub when Diana was shot, and saw you run out and drive away in the unmarked police cruiser. We have been one step behind you the entire time.

"When we went to Diana's apartment, we found the other tapes of Kane and Raymond. Once we evaluated them and heard your interaction with her, we knew that you played no role in any illegal activities. In fact, she left notes to go along with the tapes, specifically saying that you were not involved. We have also been monitoring the police radio channels and knew there were some dirty cops involved besides Renaldy."

"Looks like we were a little late." The other agent looked down at Ray's body with a grimace. "Too bad it had to end with Raymond dead instead of being handed an indictment. I guess his nephew will have to stand in his place. I'm sure the prosecuting attorney will have a lot of questions for you."

"Fuck you," Kane replied as the Metro police cuffed him to escort him to the police wagons that were parked outside.

A paramedic tended to Antoinette, who still lay next to Victor, unconscious. She was barely alive. The medics stabilized her as best they could and put her on the stretcher. A part of Victor felt hurt that she wanted him dead, but a part of him wasn't surprised. He had not been a good husband, but she knew the type of nigga he was when they hooked up. Shit, he tried to kill a nigga over her in the very beginning, what the hell did she expect? A deacon of a fuckin' church?

As the FBI removed a teary-eyed Renaldy in handcuffs, the homicide investigation team wrapped up the final photos of Raymond's body. Eventually the coroner's office scooped Ray up, wrapped him in a black vinyl body bag and zipped the bag closed. Quincy watched as the darkness of the bag enveloped Ray's face. *He is finally where he is meant to be,* Quincy thought, *in hell, making good on his contract with Lucifer.*

"So what about me and Ricky?" Victor said nervously to the FBI agents.

"What about you two? From everything I read and heard so far, you aren't involved in this investigation. Just stay close by so that we can ask you and your associate questions when the time comes."

"Quincy, I have to thank you for taking this vital evidence and protecting it with your life. What you did will ensure that Diana didn't die in vain." The agent extended a hand to shake Quincy's.

Once the crime scene was clear of badges, Quincy walked over to Victor and Ricky, who sat drinking at the end of the conference table.

K. Roland Williams

"So where does this leave us, Victor?" Quincy asked.

"That's a good question, Quincy. You showed some serious balls, standing up to Raymond and his crew. You know what they would have done to you once they got the wire, right?"

"Yeah, I know what they would have done." Quincy sat down in one of the tall, black leather chairs next to Ricky, who was dozing off.

"I'm sorry about Antoinette, hopefully she will be okay."

"She's a strong black woman," Victor said, staring out into space as he sipped his cognac. "She will be just fine."

"So what about you and me ... is our business finished?"

"I don't know, Quincy ... a woman I know told me that you can sing. We are looking for a soloist to be our second R&B act on the label."

"Well, then maybe we need to talk some more." Quincy pointed at the glasses and the bottle of cognac. "Can I have a glass of that good shit? It's been a hell of a weekend."

"Knock yourself out, Quincy."

K. Roland Williams

e p i l o g u e

Two months later ...

Q moved to the beat of the slow tempo track in the sound booth, feeling every note of the music. The hook was catchy and it sounded like it could be a hit right away. Q looked through the glass and watched Victor adjusting the levels on the large soundboard. The sliders began to move by themselves as he shifted the board to self adjust. Victor gave Q the thumbs up to let him know that he sounded great out there in the control room.

Quincy smiled a confident smile as he continued to hit perfectly toned notes into the Shure microphone. He focused intently on the song and could not believe that his fantasy was actually becoming a reality. Victor stopped the music and spoke into the mic, asking Quincy to come out for a minute and take a break.

"Yo, Vic, what's the problem? It didn't sound good?"

"No, you sounded great. I just wanted to show you something real quick. I figured you would want to see

K. Roland Williams

this ASAP."

"A'ight, what's going on?"

Victor opened up a large box that had the letters ASCAP on the outside. Q's first single was complete. His song had been properly recorded, mixed and mastered. The cover art was hot, and Q was tentatively scheduled to hit Baltimore's *"Fat Morning Show"* to be interviewed by Mark Clark in a few days. He was also scheduled for a telephone interview with Donnie Simpson to talk about his upcoming tour with several other hot male vocalists. Q was clearly on his way to his dream, and this time it was the real damn deal. He smiled at the cover art on the CD and thanked Victor for actually giving him a chance after all that they had gone through.

"I want to thank you, Vic. I would never have seen this day if you didn't give me the opportunity."

"Well, I said I owed you, didn't I? Besides, Antoinette was right all along, you can sing your ass off." Victor gazed over the final copies of Q's first single, satisfied with the entire project.

"Do you think she will ever wake up from that coma she's in?"

"I really don't know, and the doctors can't say for sure, but I can tell you one thing, wherever you drift off to when you're asleep like that, best believe she is plotting and scheming up some devious, foul shit. She always has to have the last word."

They continued to look at Q's CD cover. His actual

moniker would simply stay *Q*, a simple yet effective name for an artist. The title was gold on a white background, written in a fancy script and stood clearly next to a picture of Q sitting in a luxury penthouse suite—his own—lounging on a plush black leather chaise looking up at a woman who stood in front of him, barely dressed. His diamond *Cut Throat* necklace dangled past his chest.

    The title of the album was *"In the Key of Q,"* and that worked quite well for Quincy. He had survived a bunch of bullshit and come out smelling like a rose, and had done shit his way. Yes, the title fit him perfectly.

K. Roland Williams

ORDER FORM

Triple Crown Publications
PO Box 6888
Columbus, Oh 43205

Name: _____

Address: _____

City/State: _____

Zip: _____

TITLES	PRICES
Dime Piece	$15.00
Gangsta	$15.00
Let That Be The Reason	$15.00
A Hustler's Wife	$15.00
The Game	$15.00
Black	$15.00
Dollar Bill	$15.00
A Project Chick	$15.00
Road Dawgz	$15.00
Blinded	$15.00
Diva	$15.00
Sheisty	$15.00
Grimey	$15.00
Me & My Boyfriend	$15.00
Larceny	$15.00
Rage Times Fury	$15.00
A Hood Legend	$15.00
Flipside of The Game	$15.00
Menage's Way	$15.00

SHIPPING/HANDLING (Via U.S. Media Mail) $3.95 1-2 Books, $5.95 3-4 Books add $1.95 for ea. additional book

TOTAL $_____

FORMS OF ACCEPTED PAYMENTS:
Postage Stamps, Institutional Checks & Money Orders, all mail in orders take 5-7 Business days to be delivered.

ORDER FORM

Triple Crown Publications
PO Box 6888
Columbus, Oh 43205

Name: _____

Address: _____

City/State: _____

Zip: _____

TITLES	PRICES
Still Sheisty	$15.00
Chyna Black	$15.00
Game Over	$15.00
Cash Money	$15.00
Crack Head	$15.00
For The Strength of You	$15.00
Down Chick	$15.00
Dirty South	$15.00
Cream	$15.00
Hoodwinked	$15.00
Bitch	$15.00
Stacy	$15.00
Life	$15.00
Keisha	$15.00
Mina's Joint	$15.00
How To Succeed in The Publishing Game	$20.00
Love & Loyalty	$15.00
Whore	$15.00
A Hustler's Son	$15.00

SHIPPING/HANDLING (Via U.S. Media Mail) $3.95 1-2 Books, $5.95 3-4 Books
add $1.95 for ea. additional book

TOTAL $_____

FORMS OF ACCEPTED PAYMENTS:
Postage Stamps, Institutional Checks & Money Orders, all mail in orders take 5-7
Business days to be delivered.

ORDER FORM

Triple Crown Publications
PO Box 6888
Columbus, Oh 43205

Name: _____

Address: _____

City/State: _____

Zip: _____

	TITLES	PRICES
	Chances	$15.00
	Contagious	$15.00
	Hold U Down	$15.00
	Black and Ugly	$15.00
	In Cahootz	$15.00
	Dirty Red *Hardcover Only*	$20.00
	Dangerous	$15.00
	Street Love	$15.00
	Sunshine & Rain	$15.00
	Bitch Reloaded	$15.00
	Dirty Red *Paperback*	$15.00
	Mistress of the Game	$15.00
	Queen	$15.00
	The Set Up	$15.00
	Torn	$15.00
	Stained Cotton	$15.00
	Grindin *Hardcover Only*	$10.00
	Amongst Thieves	$15.00
	Cutthroat	$15.00

SHIPPING/HANDLING (Via U.S. Media Mail) $3.95 1-2 Books, $5.95 3-4 Books add $1.95 for ea. additional book

TOTAL $_____

FORMS OF ACCEPTED PAYMENTS:

Postage Stamps, Institutional Checks & Money Orders, all mail in orders take 5-7 Business days to be delivered.

ORDER FORM

Triple Crown Publications
PO Box 6888
Columbus, Oh 43205

Name: _____

Address: _____

City/State: _____

Zip: _____

		TITLES	PRICES
		The Hood Rats	$15.00
		Betrayed	$15.00
		The Pink Palace	$15.00
		The Bitch is Back	$15.00

SHIPPING/HANDLING (Via U.S. Media Mail) $3.95 1-2 Books, $5.95 3-4 Books
add $1.95 for ea. additional book

TOTAL $_____

FORMS OF ACCEPTED PAYMENTS:
Postage Stamps, Institutional Checks & Money Orders, all mail in orders take 5-7
Business days to be delivered.